RODD
10/12
23 11 012

PETERBOROUGH LIBRARIES

Also by Tom Fletcher

The Leaping
The Thing on the Shore

THE RAVENGLASS EYE

TOM FLETCHER

Jo Fletcher
BOOKS

First published in Great Britain in 2012 by

Jo Fletcher Books
an imprint of Quercus
55 Baker Street
7th Floor, South Block
London
W1U 8EW

ISBN 978 1 78087 000 7 (PB)
ISBN 978 1 78087 001 4 (EBOOK)

10 9 8 7 6 5 4 3 2 1

Typeset by Ellipsis Digital Limited, Glasgow

Printed and bound in Great Britain by
Clays Ltd, St Ives plc

For Jake

Shortly after my grandma died, I had my first waking dream. Since then I have had them frequently. And when I say 'waking dream', that's not what I mean, not really, because several times I have found out later that they're not dreams, but visions, small windows in space through which I have unwittingly, unintentionally, observed certain happenings that should have been invisible to me. On that first night I lay awake in bed and saw a small box hidden beneath a pile of old odd shoes in the airing cupboard. I saw that inside the box there was an envelope, and that inside the envelope were several old love letters that my granddad had sent her during the war. I got out of bed and found the letters exactly where I'd envisioned them to be. Soon afterwards, I got rid of most of my belongings and set out for West Cumbria.

That was the first vision, the first seeing. I am unable to explain this phenomenon, this *seeing*, and, if I'm being completely honest, I'm unsure really of its existence at all, because nobody else knows about this, only me, and when the entire knowledge of something is held within you and you alone, as far as you know, then it is very difficult to be sure of it, if you are a thoughtful and realistic person, as I am, or, at least, as I try to be.

PART ONE

Dearest Edith,

I hope to God this letter finds you well. It is one of my greatest fears that something should happen to you while I am out here; it would be a cruel trick of the kind that some of us have come to expect from this world. I miss you terribly, which is only right and proper but by Hell it is difficult.

I will tell you the minimum about my life out here, because in all truth it is as miserable as you might expect. Everybody is tired and pining for their loves. And everybody is scared. But I have met some good men, and we keep our spirits up by talking about coming home. Imagining this all to be over, and us seeing all of your pretty faces again. Not only seeing your face, but knowing that it wont be for just a short while. After this, Edith, we will never spend a night apart again, not if I have anything to do with it.

As I say, I dont want to write about the war — the mud and the blood and the weapons. Suffice to say, I myself am well and able to write you, and as long as I can write to you, then I shall.

I want to tell you about the place I grew up in. I have told you before of the fondness I feel for my home — the little village of Gosforth. But it makes me feel better to write about happy times I spent there and thereabouts, and perhaps it will cause you some comfort also. It helps to remember what we are fighting for, I find. In a way. Of course the world changes fast, but that is one of the most appealing aspects of Cumberland — it feels unchanging in a lot of ways.

South of Gosforth, there is a valley called Wasdale. We — my brothers and sisters and I — used to go there on our bicycles when we were young and swim in the clean, fresh lake of Wastwater. I remember hot summer days when the sun was truly bright and the paths were dappled in light beneath the tall old trees.

Sylvia was always looking after us because she was the oldest, and she would have a picnic in her basket. Just cheese sandwiches, more often than not. And when we got to the shore of the lake we would be so hot from the summer sun that we just ran right in, splashing around like children. Well, of course we were children. I forget myself. The sun shone down on the shores of the lake, and the water looked so blue, and the mountains around it were so vibrant, covered in green grass and purple heather. There was a little island we could wade out to — just a large, smooth rock, really — that we called Seagull Island. On the far side of Seagull Island the water was a lot deeper and we could practise our diving. People say that Wastwater is a bottomless lake — you can believe it when you're on its edge.

I would like to take you there, Edith, and go swimming with you. Just the two of us . . .

CHAPTER ONE

Phillip is sitting at the bar, having eaten his Cumberland sausage and mash, and he is on his second Black Sheep. For some reason I find it difficult not to observe him. Every time the kitchen door swings open I steal a glance, assess his position in the bar, his drunkenness. The truth is that he fascinates me. His brown hair, slightly too long, like a shell around the back and top of his head. His red cheeks. The beginnings of jowls. He is not fat – just saggy. He looks older than he is, I think. And I think he is in his late fifties. He wears this strange, plasticky green coat literally all the time. I have never seen him out of it. It looks very thick and hot and rubbery. It's always a bit grimy, too.

Maria is darting around behind the bar, ignoring Phillip as best as she can. She has a hard frown on and her movements are cold and brisk. She retreats into a very businesslike place inside of herself anyway when the pub's busy, as it is tonight, but even when it's quiet she'll try to find something to do that means she doesn't have to talk to Phillip.

It's Friday. All of the contractors who live here during the week have gone back to wherever they came from for the weekend, but the locals come out in force on a Friday.

I plate up two vegetarian chillis and a well-done steak and put them on the small stainless steel worktop to the right of the mammoth cooker.

Mitchell slouches through from the bar a moment later, his arms full of dirty crockery that he's collected from the tables. Mitchell is the Chip Bitch. It's his job to make sure that there's always chips ready, to assemble the starters and desserts, to sweep up and wash up, that kind of thing. Everyone's been through the Chip Bitch rite of passage – it tends to be the first job for everyone around here. He's a nice boy, if dopey. But then show me a fifteen-year-old boy who isn't dopey.

'Two chips with those,' I say, pointing to the food. 'The cyclists in the far corner.'

'Aye aye, Edie,' he says, saluting. 'I think we're taking off.'

I nod, turning back to the cooker as he shovels chips into bowls. *I think we're taking off* is what Mitchell says when it's starting to get really busy. The time between now and the serving of the last meal of the night will more or less just disappear completely, and I won't remember any of it.

We stop serving food at nine so I'm out in the bar myself by half-past. Mitchell's still doing the washing up, but he's paid by the hour so I don't feel too bad.

The Tup is an old pub, and a good one. Maria's always getting guest ales in and keeps a good range of whiskies behind the bar. There's an open fire. Soft upholstery. Wooden beams adorned with horse brasses. One thing I don't like is the taxidermy – foxes, pheasants and squirrels in glass cases up on the walls – but they've been there since before Maria bought the place and I don't think she'd feel comfortable getting rid. The place could do with a good jukebox, but maybe the regular clientele wouldn't agree. I've got my stereo in the kitchen, and a collection of reggae CDs given to me by the previous chef who was ditching all of his stuff to go and live on a houseboat. He lived in the caravan before me so I can't imagine he really owned that much.

When Mark showed me around the place, he gestured at the CDs. 'What West Cumbria needs,' he declared at the time, 'is a bit more black.'

I wasn't sure what to make of that then, and I'm still not sure now. I've never forgotten those words, though. I don't know why.

When the pub is busy like this you can't talk to Maria. And you can't ever say that you're talking with Phillip, either – he just listens in to other people's talk, and then snarks at them like a nasty old dog that can't help itself yapping. So I talk to Don, who's sitting next to Phillip, which is unfortunate, but then this is a public house, after all, and like Grandma used to say, trying to avoid people you don't like is a kind of cheating.

Don is a small, hunched man with a droopy nicotine-stained moustache and big red veiny nose. Like Phillip, he has his tea here at every night.

'How's Mags doing, Don?' I ask.

He purses his lips beneath the moustache and shakes his head. 'Same as ever,' he says. 'Sometimes I think she's making a bit more sense, or she's a bit happier, but then she . . . it goes away again. I don't know if I'm helping her. I'm thinking of getting her – y'know. Having her moved somewhere.'

'I'm sure she appreciates what you do for her. Looking after her. Taking her Unsworth's custard tarts.'

'Aye! Them's about the only thing that's sure to get a smile out,' Don says. 'But I don't know if I can do it, lass. It's hard. She can't even get out of bed any more. And I don't know if she knows me all the time, y'know.'

'I'm sure she does,' I say.

'Thanks, Edie. I hope so. Sometimes it's hard to know what's best for a body.'

'Yeah,' I say, 'it is.'

'Another perfect steak tonight, mind,' he says as if that wasn't a non-sequitur, and he raises his pint to me.

'I'm glad you liked it.'

Don has steak every night, well done, with chips and peas. He finishes the pint and puts the glass down on the bar. 'I'll see yer tomorrow,' he says. 'I'd better get back to 'er indoors.'

'Goodnight, Don,' I say. 'See you tomorrow.'

'Night, Don!' Maria shouts.

Phillip doesn't do or say anything until Don's gone. And then he speaks. 'Mags isn't ill, you know,' he says in a low voice, 'she's just a hypochondriac. A drama queen. It was all before you came here, Edie, but she used to pretend to be a clairvoyant or a medium or some such, all glass beads and incense and all that nonsense: shouting fits and wailing and speaking in tongues. People fell for it, of course, because people are morons. Used to call her the Eye. If you're being kind you could say she was a madwoman, but really she was just a charlatan, and a highly-strung one at that.'

'I know the stories, Phillip, but she's mentally ill. And anyway, there's no reason not to feel sympathy for her or Don.'

'It's her own fault she's not well. Lying in bed all day? No wonder she's so fat. It's a wonder the bed can hold her. She needs to get up and do some exercise. That might sort her brain out a bit.'

'Saying one thing after another isn't the same thing as making an argument, Phillip. Just stop—'

I'm saved from having to talk to the dick further by the

front door banging open again and John Platt Senior blowing in out of the wet. He clumps over to the bar and lays his gnarled old hands out on the sticky wood, apparently oblivious to the tacky puddles of spilled beer. But then he probably can't feel anything as insignificant as spilled beer with those hands. They are like two root vegetables, yanked up from the soil and not yet washed. His nails are thick and brown with dirt and his skin is as tough and tanned as the leather of Maria's old jacket. Water runs off his threadbare blue baseball cap and down over his gaunt, ageless face. He wears a grubby green boilersuit and wellies. He brings with him the particular smell of cow muck and hay and horses.

'Double whisky please, Maria,' he says. He takes off the baseball cap and only then do I see that his hands are shaking slightly.

Maria pauses almost imperceptibly – it's not like John Senior to drink, is why – but doesn't question him.

'I'll have a whisky and lemonade, Maria, please,' I add. 'While you've got the good stuff down.'

Phillip holds his nose behind John's back and wafts his free hand in front of his face. He always does this when John Platt comes in. He explained once that it's a joke, because John smells of cowshit, but he doesn't understand that nobody else really sees it as a joke. Another thing that Phillip doesn't understand is that even if John does smell of farms, it doesn't matter.

'Alright, John,' I say.

'Edie, lass,' he replies, nodding at me.

'Alright, John,' Phillip says.

'Right,' John says, but he doesn't look at Phillip.

Phillip pulls another face and drinks deeply from his pint.

'It's been a while,' Maria says.

'Aye,' John says. 'Been busy.'

'Busy on the farm?' Phillip asks, clumsily slamming his glass back onto the bar.

'Aye,' John says, frowning briefly, still not looking at Phillip.

Then silence. John is never that talkative, but tonight, what with him drinking, and his hands shaking, the silence feels less like just silence and more like waiting. I mean, as if the silence is a prelude to something important, or something bad.

Maria places the whisky on the bar. 'You're drinking, John,' she says eventually.

'I am tonight, lass, aye.'

'What's wrong?' I ask.

'Oh,' he says, a deep sound, a weary sound. 'Found something right nasty over on the farm.'

Maria finishes dispensing the lemonade from the 'fizz tap', and holds the glass out to me. I'm looking at John, waiting for him to elaborate, and Maria's looking at John too, and for a long moment she just holds the whisky and lemonade and it's hanging in the air, and then I remember to take it off her.

'What was it?' I prompt him. 'Are you okay?'

'Oh, aye, I'm right,' he says. 'Just a speck worried, like.'

'What did you find?' Maria asks.

'Found th' dog,' John says, and falls silent again. He lifts his glass to his mouth but his hand is shaking so much that he has to put it back down again. 'Th' dog,' he says, 'all spread about. Pinned out, like, slit down the middle and pinned open.' He shakes his weathered head. 'La'al Girt. Poor old girl.'

'Oh no,' Maria says. 'Oh, John – what happened to her? Who would have done that?'

John just shakes his head again. The deep creases in which his eyes nestle fill with moisture. He roots around in the inside pocket of his boilersuit and withdraws a clutch of Polaroid photographs.

'Nice to see that not everybody is in mindless thrall to modern technology,' Phillip says. John ignores him, but I meet his eyes and give him a look and Maria shakes her head at him. Phillip shrugs.

John places the pictures face down on the bar. 'Don't look if you're squeamish,' he says.

Maria puts her hand out and then withdraws it again. 'John,' she says, 'what do you mean, split down the middle? Pinned out?'

'Oh aye,' John says, 'some bugger'd done it, like. Gullet

to arse. Skin peeled off to the sides and pinned down, like a tarp.'

Maria puts her hand to her own mouth, her face pale. 'Oh John,' she says, again, her voice muffled by her hand. She gestures to the Polaroids. 'Did you take these?'

'Aye,' John says, 'for the police.'

'Have they been out?' Maria asks.

'Aye,' John says, 'they came out today. Millom lads. Took their own pictures in the end.' He pauses for a moment, then continues. 'Said they'll look inter it, but we all know that Girt's just a dog.'

'But still,' Maria says, hands fluttering over the still-down-turned Polaroids, 'the way it's been done – they must be interested in that.'

John shrugged.

Maria measures John another whisky and puts it in front of him.

I pick the pictures up from the bar and look at them, holding them close to me so nobody else has to see them if they don't want to.

The first one is just a photo of Girt's head. I have seen Girt before, running around the fields when I'm out walking: a skinny mongrel sheepdog, black and white, a friendly dog. In the slightly discoloured photo (I think John's Polaroid camera probably dates back to the sixties or something, when he was younger, if not actually young) it looks like Girt is lying on her back, the back of her head against the ground, her jaws open. Her eyes are open but only the whites are visible. Her tongue hangs out of the side of her mouth as limp, wrinkled and discoloured as a damp dishcloth.

Below her bottom jaw, you can just see the beginning of an open wound, but there the photo ends.

I wrinkle my nose.

The next photo is more disturbing. It's taken from higher up and shows Girt's whole body. As John explained, she has been slit open from just below her jaw down to between her hind legs. Horizontal cuts have been made across the torso and stomach, enabling panels of skin to be pulled over to the side, exposing the ribs and stomach muscles of the dog. Some of the ribs are missing and the stomach muscles have been forced open too, so the interior of the chest cavity is visible. It's empty. The skin that has been pulled over to the side has indeed been pegged to the ground with something.

'Oh God,' I say, my throat tight. 'These are disgusting.'

The next photo shows a close-up of one of the pegs; it's one of the missing ribs. It's covered in dried blood and a thin layer of something white. The skin through which it has been driven is all bunched up and rough around the edges. It looks torn, as opposed to cut neatly. Black and white hair sticks out from underneath it.

The next photo is from higher up still; from John's full height, I imagine, as he is quite tall. This shows all of Girt, plus the ground around her.

She lies in the middle of a big circle of scorched ground.

I put the photos back down. There are others that I can't look at. 'Did you find her organs as well?' I ask.

John shakes his head. His big hands are trembling more violently. I'm a bit shaky too.

Maria looks uncertainly at me, and then picks the photos up and goes through them herself. I watch her face as her expression darkens.

'Excuse me?' a bald, bearded man shouts from further down the bar. Maria looks up at him, puts the photos down, puts her hand on John's hand and then leaves to go and serve the guy. Phillip snatches the photos up, shuffles them rapidly and then puts them back down without saying a word.

John downs his second double whisky. His hands are shaking less now. 'John asked if you'd come over on Sunday for the burial,' he says quietly to me. His son is also called John.

'Oh,' I say, 'if you like – I mean, if it's not an imposition. I wouldn't want to intrude.'

'Not at all,' he says. 'Tell Maria thanks for the drinks. I'll leave the money with you.'

'They're on us,' I say, but he shakes his head and puts a pile of pound coins on the bar. I pick them up and force them back into his hand. Phillip watches us with a look on his face that is something like disgust. John puts the coins on the bar again. I pick them up, but this time he's moved away. He puts his cap back on and waves as he leaves the pub.

Just me and Phillip left now, for the time being.

Outside, a sound like thunder starts to build, but it's not thunder. It grows louder and louder; a roar that sees a couple of drinkers put their hands over their ears. It's a wonder the glasses aren't moving across the tables as the volume peaks.

I'm always amazed the stuffed animals don't fall off the walls. The sound, a fighter jet, screaming across the farms and the fells, fades away. They often pass over, on training manoeuvres or something I don't know. They're one of the aspects of this place that don't quite fit. They're like giant angry metal birds, something from another world, another time. But there are a lot of things around here that don't really fit – like Sellafield, or the Eskmeals weapons testing facility; incongruous features, plucked from somewhere else and then dropped like relics from the future amongst the dunes, amongst the fields.

'Sounds like John had an unhealthy relationship with la'al Girt if you ask me,' Phillip says.

'Nobody asked you fuck-all,' I say.

'Language, Edie,' he slurs. 'Young ladies shouldn't speak like that.'

I swallow the last of my drink.

'I mean, Polaroids? In this day and age.' Phillip is talking to himself now, more or less. 'What the smelly old goat wants' – he leans from his bar stool to grab something I hadn't seen from the floor – 'is one of these.'

Phillip is hefting up a large, new-looking camera bag. From it he withdraws a very nice digital SLR that must have cost a bomb. But then, he works at Sellafield, so that kind of money is probably just chickenfeed to him. He turns it on and a little red light appears; the lens revolves and extends. He turns to me suddenly and takes a photo. The flash is dazzling.

'That's it,' I say, blinking. 'I'm going. Goodnight, Phillip.'

'Goodnight, Edie,' he says, and the camera flashes again as I walk away. The words 'smelly old goat' stay with me as I re-enter the kitchen and then leave by the back door, and I wonder if Phillip maybe still thinks of himself as young. I wonder if he's deluded enough to believe that he's significantly younger than John. Or maybe he knows he's getting older, so he is trying to differentiate between John and himself, as if by calling John old, he is putting a distance between John and himself that would not otherwise have existed.

The photos have made me cold. By the time I'm back in my caravan I can feel a deep-down chill and I'm shivering. Who would do a thing like that? Poor dog. I hope she died before all that stuff was done to her. I wonder at people sometimes. Or no, I don't. I know what people are like, the awful things people can do, but most of the time I ignore it, repress it. And then something like this comes along and rubs it right in my face – it brings it all back, it reminds me of the cruelty people can stoop to. It's so *deliberate,* that's what gets me. It's not a car accident or a crime of passion. It's done deliberately and knowingly by somebody making a particular effort.

Later on, I can't sleep for vivid and unwanted memories of those photos. I sit up and perch on the edge of the bed and wrap my arms tightly around myself. Times like this I don't want to be a person any more. I don't want to be part of the human race. I don't want to be afraid of other people, and I don't want to feel guilty on behalf of them either. Right now what I want is just to be oblivious; asleep, ideally. But the pictures go round and round. The scorched circle around Girt's body is burnt into my mind's eye, and it seems to shape the process of my thinking. I'm lying back down. I can see a figure bending over Girt's body with a knife; I can see them walking around the circle, following it. There are several of them. They're dancing now, this group of killers, dancing in a circle around the corpse, and in the distance somebody plays the fiddle.

Grandma used to tell me a story about girls who went dancing on a Saturday night, and they carried on dancing through until dawn. When the sun rose and caught them still dancing on the Sunday, they were turned to stone for disrespecting the Sabbath.

I could go for that right now, in lieu of sleep – becoming a stone. I really could.

*   *   *

I wake up and lie in bed with my eyes open for a few moments and then throw the covers off. The cold sweeps in straight away, like it had been waiting, and I briefly pull the covers back over me again before getting up and grabbing for my dressing gown. My dressing gown is thick and lilac – not a colour I would have chosen for myself, but it's warm. I feel like I need to be warm.

I can hear rain on the caravan roof. The caravan amplifies the sound of rainfall somewhat but I don't mind that. I like it, in fact. It is like being in the car at night. Small and alone.

Lamp on. Kettle on. MP3 player nestled in its dock. Gil Scott-Heron playing loud. I check my phone. It's only ten past five. I suppose it means I can get into the kitchen and get started a bit earlier than normal. On another morning I would have got back into bed, but this morning I don't want to. The chill is taking a while to dissipate. I listen to the water inside the kettle bubble and boil. It sounds like wind slowly getting stronger. I make the bed and then start to get my whites together. They're called whites, but the trousers are black-and-white chequerboard, and I wear a dark green headscarf as well. Only the shirt itself is white.

Compared to my dressing gown, the kitchen whites are thin and stiff, and they fail to keep me warm. I leave the caravan and head across the small back yard of the pub.

*   *   *

There're never many breakfasts on a Sunday morning. After about half an hour I go out into the dining room and take all of the used crockery and cutlery and glasses and cups off people's tables so that I can get the washing-up under way.

'I haven't finished,' says a middle-aged man with a turkey neck and vicious eyes. He is eating muesli.

'Have you finished with this?' I ask, holding up the tomato ketchup-smeared plate that I'd just removed from his table.

'Yes,' he says, 'but I haven't finished my breakfast overall, so you shouldn't take my plate.'

'It's generally a bit more informal than that, here, in the mornings,' I reply. I put his plate back down. 'But suit your-self.'

He looks at me with his mouth open for a moment and then points at me with his spoon. 'I'm going to make a complaint about you, young lady,' he says.

'Young lady?' I say. 'Really? Come on.'

'What?'

'If you don't know, then I'm not telling you.'

I can feel his eyes on me as I gather up more plates from around the room. There's a distant *thump*, and all the cutlery in its tray rattles: Eskmeals, doing its thing. Nobody else protests, and a few guests smile and nod as if in approval.

Sunday is the one night of the week on which a visit to the Platt place is actually possible. We do lunches which go on until about six, but then we don't do evening meals. The bar remains open, but it's a night off for us in the kitchen.

The roast dinners pass by in their usual blur and I find myself on the other side of the afternoon, alone in the gleaming kitchen and slightly dazed. The day is slowly dying, the sky out there golden and orange and red beyond the trees. This is how time gets away from us, I suppose.

By the time I've changed and am heading through the trees behind The Tup, the air has taken on a bitter quality and the month feels more like November than September. Large black birds can be seen in the treetops, and their cawing rings out. It is a sound I always associate with the smell of woodsmoke, and although it is quite abrasive, it comforts me. Before long the trees thin out and give way to the bracken-coated foothills of Muncaster Fell. The Platt farm is on the far side of Muncaster Fell, but it's possible to skirt through these foothills rather than hiking over the mountain itself, and it's actually not a long stroll.

I get to the ridge – the highest point of the journey, and about halfway – from which I can see the farm. I look behind me to see that the sea beyond Ravenglass is a blaze of gold and the sun on the horizon is a great hulking red thing.

The Johns Platt are standing in the yard when I arrive. I doubt that they've been there for long, but I can easily imagine them standing in one place for hours, not talking, just looking at something and thinking. John Junior nods at me, but doesn't say anything. He's twitchy. His blue eyes are as bright as ever, though.

Girt has been wrapped in an old blanket – one she slept in, judging by how thick with matted dog hair it is – and laid in a wheelbarrow.

'We're going to bury her,' John Senior says, 'and then have a drink.'

'Give her a good send-off,' I suggest, but I don't know where the words come from – they sound like they're from a film or book or something. It's easy to accidentally say these things when something bad has happened, but the two Johns are nodding, so it can't have sounded that weird. Maybe it came out differently to how I heard it.

We set off onto the fellside.

John and John lower Girt's wrapped body into the grave, which is about three or four feet deep, and longer than it needs to be. Without saying anything, John Junior takes the wheelbarrow – the bottom of which is now smeared with blood – and heads back to the yard before disappearing around a corner. John Senior looks down into the hole. There are two shovels next to it, upright in a mound of dirt.

The silence is broken only by the persistent cawing from the trees. Before us the ridge slopes upwards, becoming the spine of the mountain. In the light of the sunset, the crags round here turn pink.

I hear John Junior returning – it's difficult not to; the wheelbarrow is shaking so hard it sounds like it's tearing itself apart as it rolls over the bumpy surface of the yard. It's no surprise that it's protesting so loudly; John's upended a sandstone gatepost into it. He's bringing a third shovel too. The stone rests across the front and back edges of the barrow, making it difficult to manoeuvre. I expected him to struggle pushing it up to us, but he doesn't slow down at all.

I am about to ask how we'll get the stone into the hole, which I presume is the intention, but before I can say a word they have each taken an end and lifted it clear of the wheelbarrow. They don't grunt, or appear to strain at all; it's as if they are just carrying a rotten old plank between them, not a lump of solid stone bigger than either of them.

'Make sure it don't land on her head,' says John Senior, as they move around to the top of the grave.

'Do you want me to—?' I start, but then, with what looks like a sudden lapse of control, John Junior drops his end of the stone as he reaches the side of the hole.

I close my eyes so as to avoid seeing the stone crush Girt's skull, and let a brief, high shriek escape.

There is a wet thud.

When I open my eyes I see that the gatepost landed squarely in the space just past Girt's head. Exactly where it was meant to land. The Johns are both shovelling soil back into the grave already. I join in.

Once we are done, the top half of the gatepost protrudes from the turned earth like a standing stone. I walk around it so that it stands between me and the woods, The Tup, Ravenglass, the sea, the last light of the sun. It is black against the darkening blue night sky. A thin red line still lies on the horizon. From this angle I see that the gatepost still bears an old, rusted metal bolt, for hanging a gate on. It is gnarled and weathered and organic-looking, like a branch, or like a horn.

The farm consists of a low stone-built farmhouse, a grey barn, a couple of open metal sheds, the yard, some other outbuildings, including a milking parlour, and the surrounding land. There is a Land Rover and a tractor in the yard, and some other vehicles and machines in the sheds. The surface of the yard is uneven and puddled – it's probably never completely dry.

I have never been inside the farmhouse before. The kitchen is a mess: a muddy stone floor, a table piled high with paperwork and unopened envelopes, wet clothes slung over a chipped cream Aga to dry. The air is warm and smells just like the yard: cow muck and hay.

They kick off their wellies and I follow suit, removing my trainers. John Senior opens a cupboard containing a lot of unlabelled glass bottles, all of them full of red liquid. He pulls one out and I see that the bottom of the bottle is packed with small, spherical objects.

'Sloe gin?' I ask, and John nods and smiles, grabs three small glasses from another cupboard and leads the way through into the living room. 'Get the light, Edie,' he says.

I flick the light switch. The living room is probably quite big, but it feels small; every wall is covered with shelves, and every shelf is loaded with books and documents ranging in size from flimsy paperbacks through to things that look like multi-volume encyclopaedias. Many of them look genuinely old, with embossed covers, all dark red or brown or navy blue or black. Lots of spines are hanging off, or have been lost.

There are discarded jumpers draped over the backs of armchairs, empty mugs all over the place, a computer with a tin of Roses next to it, a few framed pictures hanging on the rare bits of wall that are not already obscured behind shelves. The pictures are of farm animals or old farm machinery. The one that makes a real impression is a big, intricate black- and-white drawing of a shire horse pulling a plough, pen and ink, maybe, hanging above a fireplace. There's a fire laid, but not lit. Ash from previous fires has drifted out to cover the rug and the books on the floor nearby. The mantelpiece is covered in books too, of course. The fireplace is tiled with lovely deep-red tiles.

'I like reading,' John Senior says.

'Yeah,' I say. 'So I see.'

John Junior has cleared a small round table and is pouring the sloe gin. He hands his father and me a glass each and lifts his up. 'To Girt,' he says. He always sounds a bit strange when he speaks, as if his voice has dried up a bit since the last time he spoke.

We raise our glasses and repeat his words. The gin is sweet and thick and sharp, like cough medicine. As John pours another round his father gets back up again and takes a box of matches from the mantelpiece. He lights the fire, and the flames blossom gladly, as if they had just been waiting for the opportunity.

I can't help but notice that more or less everything in the room is coated with a thin layer of dust, and that the one window is filthy.

I expect John Junior to at least talk to me, seeing as I'm here at his invitation, but he doesn't; he doesn't even make eye-contact. He just stares into the fire and drinks his gin and strokes his beard. He's a very pale young man, and very thin. His father starts talking about Girt, about Girt's mother, the litter of puppies she came from, how one of them ended up dying in the slurry tank, other stories about dogs, about the dogs on his parents' farm, about how they treated animals differently back then, less like pets, less like humans, and more like commodities or tools.

I wake up slowly, and realise that I'm still at the farm, still in the Johns' nest. My face feels sticky from the sugar in the gin, and I feel as if the gin has coated my brain too. The only light in here now is coming from the fire. My neck is burning, as if I've slept in an awkward position, which I probably have. I see that a glass of sloe gin has fallen from my fingers and spilled all over my leg.

It's only as I'm getting up that I realise John Senior is still in the room. I thought I was alone. He looks different, smaller somehow, and sunken, as if the piles of books around him have swollen up and are swallowing him down. He is so still that he looks like a wooden carving rather than a man. His eyes are open, gleaming orange in the firelight. I wonder if he is asleep with his eyes open. His face is wet.

'You off, lass?' he asks, turning his head to face me.

'Hi John,' I say. 'I wasn't sure you were awake.'

'Aye, I'm awake. Don't sleep much these days.' He turns his face back to the fire.

'What's wrong?' I ask. 'Have you been crying?'

'Aye,' he says. And then he pinches the bridge of his nose and looks down and for a moment I don't know what's happening, I wonder if he's got a nosebleed or something, but then his shoulders rise and fall and his chest heaves and a weird noise comes out of him, a sob, but it sounds more strange than that, coming from such a strong quiet person, and in this room too, a room that suddenly feels less like something intentional and more like the result of years of inaction and confusion. It strikes me that John probably isn't very happy, being up here at the farm all the time on his own, or with his son, which is more or less the same thing as being on his own, probably.

I stand and watch him sob for a bit, and then I put a hand on his shoulder, and I don't really know what to do. I feel as if I can't leave any more, not now.

'Do you want to talk?' I ask, crouching down in front of him. 'Is this about Girt?'

'Something else,' he says, 'but Girt too.'

I return to my seat and let John gather himself, wiping at his eyes with his big hands.

Eventually he's able to tell me what it is that's upsetting him. 'I miss Christina,' he says, his voice breaking on his wife's name, and then he's off again, head in hands, shaking violently. I look at his feet and count four empty bottles. They're only small, but still. I'm pretty sure it's true that John doesn't normally drink; yes, he makes sloe gin, but he gives it to people at Christmas or for birthdays, that kind of thing. When he comes to the pub he usually sticks to soft drinks. So this sadness, well, it's real, of course, but it will also be augmented by the alcohol.

After a couple of minutes he continues, 'Christina died just six years ago. The Creeping Jesus got her – we'd known it was likely for about a year before that, and Girt had known too, you could tell from the way she looked at Christina. But still, when it happened—'

'Creeping Jesus?' I interjected.

'Aye – the cancer.'

'Oh right,' I say, 'sorry.'

'I miss her so much,' he says, 'but she deserved better

than me, Edie. I feel guilty for the things I've done since she passed.'

'I'm sure you haven't—'

'None of that shite,' he barks suddenly. 'You don't know yet.'

The room feels dark and dank now, despite the fire. The thought of him sitting here night after night surrounded by this clutter fills me with a kind of grim feeling, a sadness, but an uncomfortably specific one, centred as it is around him in particular. What I mean is, from now on, thinking about John will make me feel sad and so I maybe won't want to think about him too much. That's not to say I won't think about him, obviously, because that would be callous, but what I'm trying to say is that I will feel reluctant to because I'll just be picturing a man alone, crying, in an old dark house.

'After the funeral John and me, we came back here, and we just got on with things. It hit us both hard, but he didn't want to talk about it. Anyway, I started going for walks in the evenings, instead of sitting in front of the telly. I didn't want to cry in front of John or any bugger else much for that matter, but I did need to let it all out. As well, sitting in front of the telly reminded me a bit too much of her, 'cause that was what we did of a night. So I'd go out on these walks up Muncaster Fell, or along the estuary, or sometimes over the back of the fell to Muncaster Tarn. When the days got longer I went to the tarn more often, because it was a longer walk and my favourite. I used to like just sitting on a rock by the water and watching the crags in the sunlight at the end of the day.'

He falls silent for a short while, but I don't say anything. Eventually he says, 'One night I was at the tarn and from out of the trees – do you know the tarn?'

I shake my head.

'There are trees around most of it, and in the evening it gets dark under the trees, even when the sky is still blue, or pink or red – this night it was pink, I think, but it was still dark under the trees.'

He pauses again. 'Go on,' I say, after a moment.

'And from out of the trees on the far side I could hear someone laughing, and then this light floated out from the darkness and it came out over the water and the sound of laughing got closer – as if it were coming from the light, like. And the light came towards me – a big glowing ball – and settled on the grass next to my rock, and inside the light was a woman no bigger than a foot tall. And naked too. And she was laughing and smiling and – I feel bad talking like this in front of a young lady such as yerself, Edie, but she – she was brazen, if you catch my drift.'

I blink and shake my head, and I think he interprets that as 'don't worry, carry on', but I don't completely know what the shake of the head meant. I don't know what to say at all.

'I felt like I should get up and run off, but I didn't want

to. She climbed onto my arm and then up to my face and started kissing me. And then the next thing I knew she was full-sized, like, as big as a normal person, but she was still glowing and she was still naked – and, Edie, I remember thinking – and this is what I feel guilty for – I thought she was the most beautiful woman I'd ever seen.'

'Maybe it was just a hallucination,' I say.

'I went back the next night,' John says, hanging his head now, his voice deeper, and hoarse from the crying, 'and there were more of them, and they'd laugh and sing as – as it happened.'

'As what happened?'

'You know what, lass.' John can't meet my eyes and I can't tell if he's laughing now or crying again. 'With each other, with me – and me being an ugly man, and old too – I forget me own birthday sometimes, and that son of mine, he forgets it too, but these girls – they don't care how old I am . . . I don't know what Christina would say. I don't know what I'm doing, Edie. I don't want to see them any more, and I stopped going to the tarn last year, but sometimes they come here, come up to the bedroom window, and I can't keep them out.'

I look at the fire, which is dying back now and just a tumble of black coals against the hot orange embers beneath.

'I think you're tired, John, and drunk. I think you should go to bed.'

'That's why I've got all these books,' he says, waving his arm around. 'Old folk stories, like. Myths. I'm trying to learn about it all. About them. About the fey – how to stop them. I don't find out much about them but I find out a lot about a lot of other things.'

'What kind of things?'

'D'you think Christina would be angry?' he asks, as if seeking reassurance, or permission, even. I'm not sure that he heard my question. 'I just don't want to be on my own.'

'I'm sure she'd understand,' I tell him, though I'm only saying it to make him feel better. I'm not convinced she would even believe him, let alone understand.

'Thanks, lass,' he says.

'I'm going to have to go,' I say. 'I've got to do the contractors' breakfasts in the morning.'

'Aye, you get off,' he says. 'Edie, forget all of this – I'm sorry for bringing it up. And, er, if you could keep it to yourself, I'd appreciate that.'

'Of course,' I say. 'Of course.'

The stars are out and bright by the time I leave the farmhouse. Like always when I'm drunk, it's when the fresh air hits me that I feel it. Everything is sharp-edged and hyperreal: too vivid, too stimulating for me – sound, sight, smell, taste, touch. Drinking short-circuits my body so that these senses hit my stomach first and make it jump. Anything can prompt vomiting, so I have to slow everything down, try not to look at too much, taking deep breaths and focusing on fixed points. Deep breaths and fixed points. I make my way across the yard, fixed first on the gate, and then the top of the ridge, the near horizon. That sloe gin was strong stuff. I didn't even drink that much of it, or at least, not that many glasses – but maybe the glasses were bigger than gin glasses are supposed to be?

It's only as I pass beneath the canopy of the trees that I remember Girt, her body spread out and profaned, desecrated. It is dark, and difficult for me to focus properly on anything, and this is when things start to spin. I'd hoped to make it back to The Tup and a toilet bowl at least, but no— I put a hand out and lean against a tree and let it come. It's the only way with me: if it's going to happen it's going to happen, and I'll feel better afterwards, no two ways about it.

The sound of me being sick is loud in the night and I feel like I can hear myself from a distance. Some detached part of me imagines I am an observer, some traveller out enjoying the starscape and the serene, mystical atmosphere of the fellside, suddenly alarmed by the horrible noise I am making.

I have my dreads tied back, thankfully.

As soon as it's all out, I start to feel less ill, if still a bit drunk. Everything stops spinning and my head clears. It's cold though: a bright, chill September night, but dark here, below the treeline – and whoever killed Girt has not been caught yet, presumably. What kind of priority is given to this kind of thing? It's a horrible killing, but it's the killing of an animal. Do the police treat it as a potential threat to humans, or is it a lesser crime – on a par with other types of cruelty to animals, or maybe damage to property?

As I walk between the trees, images flicker through my head: a dog in distress, the way they twist and whine. How did they keep her quiet? I see the knife go into the neck, and the blood, coming out quickly and willingly. I see her eyes rolling around in their sockets as easily as marbles along a tabletop.

By the time I get back I am in no mood for sleep, and I feel almost sober again. I pour myself a beer in the dark, deserted bar and listen. It's so quiet I can hear the tide out there in the estuary – and I can hear voices too, and laughter.

Gabe and his friends are still up, somewhere. I find my mobile in one of the many pockets and scroll through the contacts list until I find him. The signal is patchy here, but sometimes, like now, my phone finds it.

It rings four times and then he answers. 'Edie?' he says.

'Yeah – I just got in. Are you doing something? Have you got the console on? I don't feel like going to bed yet.'

'We're playing some stupid racing game that Billy brought round,' Gabe says. 'It's fucking awful. But yeah, come on up.'

*   *   *

At first glance, Gabe's room is a mess of DVD cases and wires, but amongst the electronic detritus, comic books and role-playing rule-books can be seen. In fact, it looks like the boys were engaged in a game of Dungeons and Dragons earlier tonight, judging by the amount of dice and scrappy sheets of paper covered in statistics scattered around. There is a desk fan whirring away in the corner of the room, stirring everybody's hair as the blades rotate.

There are four of them: Gabe, Billy, David and Ed. Two of them are wearing band hoodies: Gabe's bears the band name *In Flames* across the back of it and Ed's says *Converge*. The other two are wearing T-shirts covered in insignia that I can't decipher. All four of them are clustered around Gabe's relatively small TV, which is the only light-source in the room. The room smells of marijuana. I sit on Gabe's bed with my back against the wall. His bed is probably disgusting, but as long as I stay on top of the covers I should be safe.

'You must be keeping your mum up,' I say to Gabe.

'Nah,' he says without looking at me, 'she wears earplugs. You want a lager?'

'Go on then,' I say, after a moment. There is a part of me that knows more alcohol is not a good idea, but it is deep down and far away. Ed roots around in a carrier bag near his feet and passes me a can.

As I drink I realise that I am either too tired or too drunk to offer much in the way of conversation, but it feels good relaxing, just sitting there in the corner of the room and not having to worry about engaging. That's what I like about Gabe and his friends: they just accept. They don't wonder why you're doing what you're doing, they don't take offence, they don't ask for anything, they don't really care what you say or don't say. Their language and humour might be foul and offensive, but then, so is mine when I'm with them. And they are not unkind: that is the important thing. They might get angry or clumsy, but they are not unkind.

I watch them play the game, listen to them mutter to each other, find myself laughing at their insults and mock fury. Eventually I drift off and wake up again. There's a wet patch on the bed next to me and I recoil, but then realise that I've just dropped my can.

'Gabe,' I say, 'I'm heading off. Thanks for the drink, Ed.'

'No problemo,' Ed says.

'See you tomorrow, Edie,' Gabe says.

'Yep,' I say, 'tomorrow. See you then.'

I try to move quietly across the dark landing and down the narrow staircase to the bar. Moonlight shines through a window on the landing, which is helpful, but the steps feel flimsy beneath my feet. I can feel them flexing, and with each flex comes a long creak.

I hurry through the gloomy, empty bar and into the kitchen and let myself out of the kitchen's back door.

CHAPTER TWO

'I like how they feel connected to an older time,' I say. 'The way you can touch the stones and imagine the people who put them there and the way the views must have looked back then – all of the weather those stones have seen. I like wondering what they were for as well, what ceremonies or celebrations. They always seem a bit magic.'

'Bit sentimental,' Phillip mutters. 'They were just to mark meeting places for traders – I thought everyone knew that.'

'You'd only need one stone for marking,' John says. 'Or none at all if it were a regular meet.' This is John Junior this time. He comes to the pub more frequently than his father, but he talks less. Tonight he's making an effort though – maybe he's interested in stone circles? He perked up when I mentioned them. He could be interested in lots of different things; I just don't know.

Phillip doesn't respond to what John said. He acts as if

he wasn't paying attention, as if he didn't hear – he always does that: says his piece and then ignores any comeback.

'My grandma always used to say they were people turned to stone for being wicked,' I say, 'for doing something evil, like dancing on a Sunday.'

Phillip snorts into his pint, but we ignore him.

'I like the one at Castlerigg,' I continue. 'That's the best I've seen in a while.'

'Greycroft,' John says, 'there's a good one at Greycroft.'

'Where's that?' I ask.

'No distance – Seascale way, next to Sellafield. It's good. I'll take you tomorrow.' He's blushing. 'If you want, I mean.'

'Oh,' I say, 'yeah, of course – I mean – I didn't know there was one there.'

'Aye,' he says, 'not many do.'

I suddenly feel a bit self-conscious so I drink deeply from my pint in an effort to hide my face. When I put the glass back down Maria is just moving off to serve somebody else, but we make eye-contact and she raises one of her carefully plucked eyebrows and smiles slightly. The women around here all think John Platt Junior is a bit of a catch. There's not much competition, to be honest.

The door opens and Don tramps back in and resumes his position at the bar. He's wet. On the road, and on the beach, and across the estuary, rain is falling. He picks up the pint he'd started with his food and takes a gulp. 'All done,' he shouts to Maria.

'Thanks, Don,' Maria shouts back.

'It's raining,' Phillip says.

Don just looks at him blankly. 'Aye?' he says eventually.

'Well, the plants don't need watering if it's raining, do they?'

Don maintains his blank look, a kind of confused and innocent expression. It is a very effective defence.

What Don does is; every day he comes and has his tea at The Tup, but he doesn't pay for it. Instead, he waters all the plants in the pub grounds, whether they need it or not, whether it's raining or not. He used to water the plants and then come in for his food, but over the past few months his routine has started to vary, and sometimes he comes in and has his tea before watering the plants. Sometimes he is out there watering the plants long after it has gone dark. Like Phillip, he always orders the same thing – though he eats steak every night, whereas Phillip always eats sausages. Maria used to ask Don to pay for his food, as it's part of Mitchell's job to maintain the grounds, and Don did pay for his food when asked, but he continued to water the plants as well, until it got to the point where Maria felt too bad to ask for money any more.

Naturally, Phillip finds this arrangement deeply contemptuous.

I don't believe that Don is being deliberately difficult or obtuse or somehow tricky; I think that he genuinely believes that it's his duty to water the plants, whatever the weather, and that his evening meal is part and parcel of the deal.

He doesn't eat the chips, but wraps them in tinfoil and takes them home to Mags.

One moment I'm slicing a tomato, one of many, and the next I'm watching John Senior sitting on the shore of some small, calm body of water and he's looking out towards some trees and the sun's coming up and he's watching the trees intently, as if waiting for something to come out from beneath them. Then the vision is over and I feel a biting pain and I see that the knife has sliced through my finger as well as the tomato while I was distracted and unseeing.

'Shit,' I say, 'shit, shit, shit.' It is a deep cut and quite bloody, and now I can't use this stupid tomato. I turn on the cold tap and hold my bleeding finger beneath it until the water starts running clear again, and then I dig out the first-aid box, stick a blue plaster on, and throw all of that perfectly good tomato away. I start chopping some fresh ones, trying to ignore the pain.

John parks up just off the A595, the dry dust of the lonnin clouding up around the wheels of his Land Rover and settling on the already dirty vehicle. My cut finger is itchy.

'You know this path?' he asks.

'No,' I say, 'I thought it was private down here.'

'Some of it is,' he says. 'Some of it is Simon Halliwell's land. But the Halliwells won't mind me.'

'Because you're a farmer?'

'Aye,' he says, 'well, we're on good terms, like.'

He notices me fiddling with the plaster on my finger and looks down at my hand. 'What happened there?'

'Slicing tomatoes this morning,' I say. 'My hand slipped.'

'Deep?'

'Yes.'

He turns off the engine and we both get out of the car. The green of the dykes and trees is just beginning to fade. There are clouds gathering in the sky.

We walk without speaking, but it's not awkward. Silence is John's inclination. When he comes into the pub he usually sits on his own. If you see him in the village or at the shops in Seascale he nods, but rarely says anything – barely even looks at you sometimes. In all honesty, the main reason I accepted his invitation was some kind of sense of obligation; this man who never asks anybody to do anything suddenly asked me to do something, and I would have felt pretty bad if I'd said no.

The noise of the traffic on the A595 is deadened by the tall hedgerows that we're walking between, and the only other things to hear are the sheep baa-ing in nearby fields and birdsong from the occasional copse of trees that we pass.

After about fifteen minutes the lonnin forks, but the junction is surrounded by trees so that it's not possible to see very far down either route. John takes the left-hand path and I follow his lead. We round a corner and find ourselves standing before a mansion.

'Oh my God,' I say, 'I didn't know this was here – how did we not see it on the way?' But even as I ask I realise that the tall, dark trees around the building completely shroud it.

John turns around, his face creasing at the corners of those bright blue eyes. I think he's smiling, but it's not always possible to tell because his beard's quite thick.

The house is derelict – it's immediately obvious, even before you notice the broken windows, the gigantic rusty padlock on the front door, the graffiti. It just has that abandoned air about it. It looks like it has grown over time, with extensions at either end, though even they could be more than a hundred years old. The central part is sandstone, naked but for a coating of pale green lichen. The windows of that section are tall and thin, like church windows. The extensions – one of which is as large as two good-sized houses, the other as big as one good-sized house – are both rendered and have the more modern rectangular windows with wooden frames. There is one huge double door in the front which, being peaked, is as reminiscent of a church building as the oldest windows.

'What's it called?' I ask.

'Newton Manor,' John replies. 'It's been empty for years. Nirex bought it up. This is where the dump would've been.'

'The nuclear waste dump?'

'Aye. Didn't happen, but they've still got the manor, though done nowt with it.' He gestured around.

I go up to the house. It looks as if the doors have been kicked in at one point; the original lock is long gone and the padlock is the only thing holding them closed. There's a gap between them of about an inch, through which I can see a few empty lager cans lying on the tiled floor and some floral wallpaper peeling off the wall.

'Can we get inside?' I say, turning around.

John's eyes shift from me to the building and back again. 'We shouldn't,' he says. 'Trespassing.'

'I suppose.' I step away from the doors and wander down to the far end of the building, where I can see a sturdy lean-to. It is open, but there's a big clump of creepers hanging down over the doorway, so I have to duck to get inside.

It's still full of stuff: an old hand-push lawnmower with a cylinder blade; a workbench covered in rusty metal implements, tobacco tins and jars full of nails; stacks of newspapers from – I check the dates – the mid-eighties. The door can't have been left open all this time or this stuff would have deteriorated to nothing; it must have been forced open relatively recently. The walls are lined with wooden shelves that are stacked with toolboxes and plant-pots and rags. Strange bundles that look like giant pupae hang from the beams of the low ceiling, but on closer inspection they're blankets, rolled up and tied and then hung from hooks. Like everything else, they're thick with cobwebs. It's like being inside a sepia photograph. Even the blue plaster on my finger looks brown. The cut is maddeningly itchy now. I keep scratching at the skin around it and the plaster's getting loose.

John's standing behind me, looking over my shoulder. 'Do you know what those blankets would've been for?' I ask him.

'No,' he says. He picks up a wooden mallet and scuffs the floor and a cloud of dust blossoms. 'Wonder why they left everything.'

Leaving the lean-to, John points to a strange mound of greenery opposite. It is too perfectly semi-spherical to be a natural thing, but nothing of the actual structure can be seen through the foliage. He goes over to it and parts the ivy that covers it like hair. He disappears inside. I follow him.

The only light comes in through the entrance, so it's quite hard to see anything, but as my eyes get used to the dark, I see the curved walls of the igloo-like building are formed by carefully arranged pieces of slate. Some have white marks on, as if they've been struck by another stone, or maybe a piece of metal. I imagine somebody sitting in here and marking time. I move forwards and my boot scuffs over something. Bending down, I find the melted-down stump of a candle; a big, thick white one. It's one of several.

'I take it this was used as an ice-house?' I ask, looking at the candle stump.

'Aye. I think so.'

'Look at all this wax. You reckon teenagers come and get it on in here?'

'Probably – anywhere out of sight. We've found some local kids at it in the milking parlour before now.'

I didn't expect John to answer the question so directly.

'Let's have a look around the back of the house,' I say.

From behind, the structure is much more complicated. There are various narrow walkways between even more late additions to the property, with large, elaborate greenhouses abutting modern sheds and outbuildings. The garden is now just a tangle of tumbledown walls and rampant foliage. A few wizened old apple trees sporting ripe fruit are visible, but they're surrounded by a thicket of brambles so dense that I can't get to them. The apples are bright amidst the gloomy greenery, and it feels like they're the only really living things in this whole place.

I climb on top of one of the most stable-looking walls, which is about two feet away from the rear wall of the oldest bit of the house. The way the garden and the grounds have been landscaped means that from the top of this wall I can see into an upper-storey window. It must have been a dark house inside, what with this wall blocking all the light.

John is standing below me in the passageway between the wall and the house. He looks nervous.

'I'm just going to look through this window,' I say, and I reach out and put my hands on the wall of the house, then lean forward to look through the window. It's actually unlocked and it opens when I push it.

'Hey,' I say, 'John, look – we wouldn't even have to break and enter; we could just enter! It might be a squeeze, but I think I could get in if I tried—'

'I don't know,' he says, 'I'm not sure, Edie. Got to get to Greycroft yet, and I need to get back to the farm before too long.'

The window opens onto a bend in a big old staircase which is carpeted. There is a panel of light making it through from somewhere else though – one of the windows round the front, presumably – which illuminates a patch of wallpaper up near the top of the staircase, maybe even on the landing. It's more of that floral stuff. Horrible.

I can't see anything else. I look and look, but it's all in darkness and my eyes aren't adjusting.

If anybody's standing looking back, they'll be able to see me clear as day.

I lean away from the window and let it fall shut again. Once you've had that thought about the darkness you can't let it go; you can't unthink it.

I make my way back through the labyrinthine warren of the gardens to the end of the house, across which a dark green vine is spreading, and meet up with John. 'You're right,' I say to him, 'let's not go inside.'

The path to Greycroft continues on the other side of Newton Manor, so we have to walk past the front of it. Now I'm conscious of all of the windows looking down on us and the urge to run is difficult to resist.

It's only when we've left the woods behind and are once again out amongst the fields that I'm able to shake the sticky feeling that darkness can give you.

The stone circle is unexpectedly wide, unexpectedly intact. The stones stand like watchmen at the land's edge. They're all even and tall in the gathering dusk and the sea breaks not far beyond, looking much as it must have looked when these stones were first put in place. Seagulls cry out as they float above, using the rising winds to hover. The green grass against my bare feet is soft and cool and it curls up around the bottom of the stones too and I can't help but imagine the stones enjoying it as I do.

About twenty yards to the north is the perimeter fence of Sellafield Nuclear Reprocessing Plant. The lights of the reprocessing plant give the sparse clouds above it beautiful orange undersides, and the darkening blue of the sky shows through. The nearest buildings aren't visible, due to an incline and a screen of tall trees, but further away the tops of strange towers and blank-looking office blocks loom like the holy architecture of some civilisation long gone or not yet here.

John lies on his back looking up at the thin clouds, his hands behind his head, and I lie down next to him in the middle of the circle. I want to say something, anything, but I'm not sure what. We don't know each other very well at all.

'It's funny, the things you can not know,' I say at last. 'This stone circle, that big old house – I didn't know about either of them.'

John doesn't say anything. I get up on my elbow and look at him. His interwoven fingers are like a pile of kindling. His eyes find mine and he smiles a little, but he still doesn't say anything.

'It's a good one,' I say, gesturing around at the grey boulders.

'Aye,' John says. He grins through his black beard. There is nothing other in the grin. It's a nice smile and that's all, and that's just right. I smile as well. John is a good man, I believe, and if I were looking for someone then right about now I'd probably put my hand out to his chest and touch it, maybe lean over him and suggest a kiss, and there's a part of me that wants to do that, but a much greater part that knows better and so I keep my hands where they are and keep smiling and look away from John at the stones and then I stand up and look out at the sea again. The sound of the sea is a gentle sweeping; as if somebody somewhere else is going around with a broom.

I'm walking around the circle. The outer side of half of the stones have an even green skin, slurry that's been sprayed over them by a muck-spreader and has then dried, but it's getting dark now, and the dark green looks black. It must have been sprayed a while since because there's none of the crap on the grass.

One of the stones even has a big, jagged scar, as if it's been knocked by something mechanical – the muck-spreader, maybe – and had a lump knocked off.

In my mind's eye I see a hand reach out and touch it. It's a clear, brief vision.

It feels like an instruction.

Breathless, I reach out myself. I haven't had a vision with such lucid meaning since seeing the box of letters that Granddad wrote to Grandma. I run my finger around the edge of the stone's wound, excitedly, clumsily, and the plaster gets caught and drops off, and pulls away the scab that was forming. Fresh blood beads and drops onto the stone. It looks too red, and I stare at it and blink: red on the black. I pull my hand away. Was that the intention? Was that what was supposed to happen?

And what will happen now?

As I step back from the stone, John calls out, 'Edie, come here a moment.' He is standing with his back to me in the middle of the circle, watching a seagull. The wind is playing with a few loose strands of his hair. He needs it cut, really, but I'm not going to say that.

He turns around and looks at me. He looks different: his eyes are different; darker somehow, more serious. The collar of his checked shirt is up around his neck. Behind him is the sea, grey and white-capped in this rising wind. The stones all around us feel like witnesses.

'Edie,' he says. He moves in and hesitantly puts his hands on my shoulders. It's as if he doesn't want to do it, but feels like he has to.

'What are you doing?' I ask.

He looks at me, somehow afraid, and opens his mouth. Then he quickly, jerkily, presses his face against mine, the bristles of his beard prickling into my chin, his lips dry and papery on my own.

I pull my head away and step backwards, swinging my arms up to dislodge his hands. 'John! What the fuck are you doing?'

'What—? Edie—? What do you—? Oh no . . .'

'What do you mean, "oh no"?'

'I thought – I meant something else. I meant for something else. Edie, I'm sorry.' His whole body is slumped, and his arms are now hanging heavily at his sides.

'I didn't think you felt like that,' I say, folding my arms, but before he can respond, a tremor runs through the ground and I stumble backwards. I get that feeling in my stomach, like when you dream you're falling, or when you're on a rollercoaster going down.

'Shit,' I hear John say as the trembling subsides, 'Jesus! Come on, Edie, let me take you home – I mean to your home. I mean I'll drop you off at the pub. I won't kiss you or anything. I'm so sorry.'

'That shaking – was that Eskmeals?'

John looks around, his head still hanging low. I don't know what he's looking for. 'Yeah,' he says at last, 'I think so. Must've been a big one.'

Silence falls. He doesn't look up.

'Come on then,' I say, 'let's go.'

'I understand if you don't want to get in the car with me,' he says, not moving.

'Let's just go, all right?'

John shakes his head. 'I'll drop you at the pub,' he repeats. He reaches out an arm as if to put it around my shoulders, but then thinks better of it.

I turn and look back at the stones before we return to the network of lanes and hedgerows. They stand out darkly against the sea, sharp and proud. As I watch, the violent roar of a jet reaches me from the north and I put my hands over my ears – the sound is more piercing outside – and look up at the black shape dividing the sky.

John drops me on the main road – the only road in Ravenglass, really. It follows the edge of the estuary and there's a grassy embankment separating the tarmac from the sand. There are metal benches and handrails on the embankment, painted bright blue.

On Friday afternoons, the weekend visitors start to appear. They pop in and out of the guesthouses, gradually busying up the village. A lot of them wear gaudy waterproof jackets and ride bikes. They're here to explore the mountains and valleys, to cycle new routes, to drag their bored children to antique fairs, to pull their jeans up high and drink pints of locally brewed beer on picnic benches outside the pubs.

The brooding lattice of the railway bridge stretches out across the estuary. There's the sound of seabirds, the smell of the sea and, thanks to the La'al Ratty steam locomotives, the smell of sulphur too.

Something is loose and I have loosed it.

The words are already there in my head when I wake up, waiting for me. It's still dark outside the caravan – not early-morning dark, which is what it normally is when I wake up, but middle-of-the-night dark. I listen out for something, for the sound that could have disturbed my sleep, but the only thing I can hear out there is the wind in the trees, which isn't anything unusual.

I look up at the ceiling and try to work out what has changed. Something has, I know it. I feel different. Imagine waking up in the middle of the night and realising you've got a new tooth in your mouth. That's not what's happened, but it's that kind of feeling, of something being different in perhaps quite an unobtrusive way, and yet it's fundamental, it's significant. Those horror films where somebody wakes up and finds out they're an amputee – they always find out by looking at the stump where they expect the limb to be and then they scream – but what do they feel before they know? I imagine they feel similar to what I'm feeling now.

After thinking about amputation I have to check my own body for any physical changes, but there's nothing out of the ordinary. As I pat myself down, checking I've still got all of my fingers and toes, the knowledge kind of sinks into me; it becomes obvious that something new – something *powerful* – is awake and hungry and *here*. Without seeing it or hearing it I know this: I know, because it is connected to me. Its mind is like a candle shining in the dark, distant reaches of my own consciousness. There is no doubt. I know it like I know when I've got a headache. Something I did or something I am brought it here, and now it is here. And I know, suddenly, in a deep and unshakeable way, that I am going to find it very difficult to get to sleep at night, thinking about it, listening out for it, wondering what it might look like when I meet it, if I ever meet it. It could be a human being, I suppose, but that candle in my head does not feel like a human candle.

Whatever it is, it is coming to me right now. The flame

is approaching through the gloom. In the way that you can hear a car getting closer, I can sense this. I don't know what the sense is – it's something new to me – but it is real.

And then I can hear it. It sounds like shoes in mud, some-body squelching through a bog. But there is no bog outside my caravan, it's paved.

The Candle has come to see me. The light in my mind is flaring ever more brightly as the sound gets louder. It's come to see me. What will it look like? Why does it make that sound as it walks? I get up out of bed and rush to the door and unlock it and throw it open.

The sound stops. The night is dark. The Tup is a great big black shape against a sky filled with silver-edged grey clouds. A light breeze whispers through the trees. As my eyes adjust I am able to make out the lines of the paving stones beyond the steps down to the ground, and details like the windows and back door of the pub.

And there, in the shadow of the back door, partially obscured by a trellis covered in some wiry old plant, is a figure of some kind, and it's the Candle, it is, it is, I *know* it is. Though I can't see it clearly. It's there, but it's shrouded in darkness, and the most I can see, courtesy of the occa-sional glimmers of moonlight, is the shape of a shoulder and the edge of one long arm. I fight the urge to slip back inside and turn the light on. I am sure that if I were to do that, the Candle would disappear.

'Hello?' I say.

The Candle bows, or, at least I think it does, judging by the dipping motion.

'Are you the Candle?' I ask.

I hear the sounds of laughter, of lots of different people laughing, the sound coming from all over, and somewhere in there is a delighted affirmation, a *yes, yes, yes, that's right!*, as if the Candle is amused and pleased by the question, or perhaps by the moniker I have given it. Some of the laughter is familiar and I wonder if the Candle has used my own memories to formulate its response, or if the sound of one group of people laughing sounds much the same as another group of people laughing. I wonder if I heard the laughter at all, or if the Candle just made it happen inside my head.

'I'm pleased to meet you,' I say.

I'm pleased you're pleased, it says, or rather, it uses other voices to say. *I'm pleased you are so receptive to me.*

'I've been waiting for something like this.'

Haven't we all.

'What are you? Why have you come to me?'

I was once a man, and as a man I performed certain rituals to make my spirit immortal. When my body was cut up and burned on that green grass, my spirit fled to the Elsewhere, where it has remained ever since. Where it has grown and changed. And you are my saviour, Edie Grace. You and your Eye.

'What?'

Your visions. You were born with a gift that you have never been in control of. Your Eye was like a beacon to me, out there in the vast and dark Elsewhere. Your Eye – your ability – gave me hope. I was able to influence what you saw, ever so slightly, and, ultimately, find a way back in.

'You showed me the letters.'

Yes.

'You made me cut myself.'

Yes.

'You told me to bleed on the stone.'

Yes. And that last act set me free. That brought me here – brought me home.

'But why didn't you do it before? I've been here for years now.'

Shaping your sight from so far away cost me so much. Even though my influence from that distance was feeble, it exhausted me to use it. It was only once I knew you were going to the stones that I could risk exerting myself so heavily; heavily enough to lead you to cut your finger. Once you were at the circle, so close to my remains, it was easier for me to suggest the touch, to cause the spilling of blood.

'But it worked.'

Yes. Though I am still weak – still just a shade. And so I have come to ask you for yet more help; yet more kindness. This time, though, I can offer you something in return.

'What do you want?'

I can offer you the visions you desire; what you want to see, whenever you want to see it. Anything here in this world is yours for the witnessing.

'I want to see Phillip,' I reply. I imagine watching Phillip and finding something out that could puncture his smugness. He's got secrets, I know it. 'But tell me – what do you want from me?'

I'm feeling the cold now. I can hear an owl softly hooting in the distance. I left my rationale behind me in the caravan and I can feel it tugging at me, trying to tempt me back inside.

I want the blood that let me in in the first place. Your blood, Edie. It has certain unique properties.

'No. No.' I step backwards, back inside. 'No. I don't want you to hurt me. No. Go away.' I close the door.

I won't hurt you. Its words are no quieter. *I ask that you give it voluntarily, and I don't ask that you give much. All magic requires a little blood; it doesn't mean that it's dangerous or destructive. I am nothing to be afraid of. Leave me a small cupful every second day and I will show you everything you want to see. As I become more firmly rooted, I will be able to do other things for you, too.*

'No.'

There is a silence. Then:

Very well.

I turn so that I'm leaning against the door, and then slide down to the floor and put my arms around my knees. There is a part of me that wants to open the door and watch the Candle leave, in order to see what it looks like. But I don't. A greater, more powerful part of me is afraid.

In lieu of really knowing, I visualise a tall man with a burnt, blackened wick protruding from his neck instead of a head. The neck is wax that has melted and re-solidified again, and wax drips are running down the side of it, hardening on his shoulders and his arms.

Chapter Three

It is after the Monday night meals, after several after-work drinks, after Maria has cleaned up and gone up to her living quarters, after I have returned to my caravan, and just as I put my headphones on to listen to some music that I have a vision. I see Phillip sitting amongst the branches of a tree. It is night-time. He has a digital camera held close to his face and is watching the screen as if he is recording something as opposed to taking a photograph. The camera is angled towards a lit window. Maria is standing in the window. She is getting undressed, unbuttoning her black shirt. Phillip in the trees and Maria in the window float together in a completely dark world.

I am aware of something breathing heavily; it could be Phillip, it could be me. I can see as much or as little detail as I want – I can zoom right out and see just the points of light in the distance, or I can zoom right in and see the moisture – rain, or maybe sweat – rolling down Phillip's face.

And then it passes.

Seeing Phillip like that, I feel as if a horrible insect is crawling up my leg and I want to shake it off, but I cannot move much. The creepy, tingling feeling spreads across me and I'm trying to jump up and shake myself, as you do when you accidentally touch something slimy and dirty, but I can't. And then, finally, I'm on my feet and jerking myself around and brushing myself down until I start to feel clean again.

Over the past few years there has been occasional talk about a local pervert. A peeping tom who's been seen sitting in trees, or crouching behind hedgerows, or lying in the bushes at the bottom of the garden. He – we assume it's a he – is only ever spotted at night, and his face is always obscured. I'd never seen him, and reports are always vague – people *think* they see a shape, something that looks like a person, but when they come back with a torch there's nothing there. People connect the stories with an unsolved murder from years back – a girl from Newcastle whose body was found in the mouth of the river. I don't know if there is really any connection or not.

But I think I know who the peeper is. I don't have proof to show anybody else, but I *know*.

I open the caravan door and sit on the step and light a cigarette. It's a cloudy night, and very dark. The ground and air are wet with a fine rain, so fine it's almost not rain at all but mist. I can't see the ground; I can't see if the Candle left any trail. I inhale the smoke and look at the building in front of me. The Tup is a large, irregular building, almost S-shaped. Maria's bedroom is near one of the ends; it looks out over a small private garden she keeps for her and her son, Gabe. Beyond that garden is a copse of trees – they were the trees I just saw, no question, and I have no doubt that Phillip was – or *is* – sitting in them, recording Maria as she takes her clothes off.

I walk around the building, trying to tread quietly, and when I come to the edge of the little garden I look up at Maria's window. The light is off now. I dart back around the corner of the building, in case Phillip is still in the trees, and watch out for any movement in that direction, but I don't see or hear anything.

It was the Candle, giving me a glimpse. A tease, showing me what it's offering – showing me that there is value in it; that Phillip does indeed have something to hide.

But the Candle scares me. It is manipulative. I don't want to make it stronger. I don't want to give it blood. Nothing that wants blood can be a good thing. Thinking back to its visit makes my stomach shrink. The sound of its footsteps – was that squelching sound its footsteps? – was horrible. I want to be inside.

Back in the caravan I get ready for bed and then root out a shoebox from the back of a cupboard. I take the lid off and shuffle through the assorted photos, letters and ticket stubs until I find a thin plastic album containing some really old pictures of my grandparents. There are letters, too, that Granddad wrote to Grandma when he was away at war.

I sit on the bed and look at one photo in particular for a long time. In it my grandparents are standing together in a garden. They are younger in the picture than I am now, and they are incredibly beautiful. I remember Herbert and Edith when they were old, when they were dying, when they were dead, but not when they were young like in the picture. I used to live with them because my dad ran off before I was born, leaving my mum – their daughter – on her own with me. And then she died – well, I'll be honest, she became an alcoholic after Dad left and that's when my grandparents took me in. Mum died drunk behind the wheel of a car when I was one, so I don't feel like I ever knew her.

I remember seeing Granddad dead in their bed. Grandma shook me awake in the middle of the night and led me by the hand into their room, all without saying a word. The shuffling of her feet was the only sound in the dark. I sat on Grandma's side of the bed and held her, her head on my shoulder, until it got light outside. She was not thin, but her skin and flesh were so soft that I felt like I could feel her bones through them. She slept on the same side of the bed for the next few years until she too died in her sleep. Maybe that's normal, I don't know, but I don't think I could bear that empty space next to me.

Every time I see a photo of an old person when they were young, an image of their old face is catapulted into my brain and the flash-bulb instancy of birth-to-death life is driven home to me and I just want to fold up and make myself oblivious.

I don't sleep, but lie awake, remembering Phillip perving on Maria through the window. It was pretty rank. My stomach contracts as I remember the details: the wetness on Phillip's face, the small bead of red light on the camera, the open curtains, the peep-show sensibility of it. The almost solid darkness, and something else – what? The heavy breathing, that was it – but it wasn't just heavy breathing; the sound was rougher, phlegmier, more laboured than breathing should be.

Yuck yuck yuck. I shake myself and shake myself and get up and walk around the caravan, and then get back into bed, and then get out and do it all again.

It's still raining, and it gets heavier as dawn breaks. I stand in the doorway of the caravan and light a cigarette as I look out. I'm not sure if I'm a smoker or not. The frequency is the important thing, I suppose: I have one every now and again, and when that 'every now and again' reaches a certain point, then I'm a smoker. Before that point, I'm not a smoker. I look at the cigarette in my hand.

The Tup has an atmosphere of still lushness; the grey sky and the constant dripping and the wild greenery just on the cusp of turning combine with the scent of woodsmoke to conjure the sense of a safe place, a warm outpost: the kind of place people might stumble upon as they travel and end up staying in for ever. Do people ever do that outside of books? I did it, I suppose.

I slip on my flip-flops and grab my caravan keys from the side, just in case the door blows shut. I walk around to the right-hand side of The Tup, the east-facing side, retracing my steps from last night, to the garden: a small square of badly kept grass bisected by a messy gravel path. I look up at Maria's bedroom window. My vision of it was accurate in every detail – the shiny black paint of the window ledge; the flaky white paint of the wooden frame; the open wooden shutters that lie flat against the outside wall and cannot be closed from inside or reached from the ground – despite the fact that I never really come round here.

Opposite the window, beyond a low drystone wall on the other side of the grass, is woodland. The trees cover the ground between here and the upwards slope of Muncaster Fell. There's nothing else – no roads between here and the fell, no houses, nothing except for the closely packed tree trunks, the canopy of branches and leaves and the deep, soft leaf-mulch underfoot. Even now, in the daylight, it's dark under there.

Again, the detail in my vision was spot-on.

I finish the cigarette as I walk over to the trees. I stub it out on the wet top of the drystone wall and brush the ash away. I keep hold of the butt as I look back up at the window, then I return to the caravan in order to get ready for breakfast.

Chapter Four

As the next few days pass, bulbous, blue-grey clouds cover the sky and moisture drips constantly from trees and gutters. It doesn't really rain, as such – it's just misty and damp. The numerous potholes in The Tup car park fill with muddy water. You can almost feel the plants and trees drinking it up, taking the opportunity to flourish one last time before autumn arrives.

It's not the *drip-drip-drip* that is breaking my sleep, or the occasional thunder echoing distantly in some midnight valley – I don't know what it is. But tonight, like the past few nights, I suddenly find myself awake and I lie here in the darkness, blinking up at the ceiling. I don't remember sleeping – obviously, nobody really remembers sleeping – but what I mean is, I am not conscious of having slept, and having been through this a few times before, I know that I am not going to go back to sleep any time soon. I am not sure I want to: there is something waiting in the back of my mind. I get out of bed and go to the window and look past the rivulets that run down the outside. The night is inviting.

I get dressed and go for a drive.

The night-time driving becomes a habit throughout the rest of September as sleeping gets more and more difficult – but it's not just that the sleeping gets more difficult; I grow to enjoy the driving itself. I like the way the lights of the car illuminate only the grey road ahead and the pale dry-stone walls on either side, and maybe some overhanging branches as well. The trees that show themselves are just changing colour, the green of their foliage shot through with orange and yellow.

That illuminated space in front of the car is all there is.

The roads twist and turn, bending suddenly, sharply and frequently. They *undulate*. It feels good to drive them at speed, but I know you shouldn't; they are too narrow for cars to pass side by side and too hemmed in by forest and rock for approaching vehicles to be visible, so you don't know that anybody else is there until they are directly in front of you, by which point there is nowhere to swerve to.

I have encountered only four or five other drivers on these roads at this time of night. Only one was driving madly, and that was last year, when I was driving back to The Tup after visiting some friends at a nearby campsite. I had a warning because the other car was old and it roared and the sound travelled clearly through the very early hours of a starry November morning. I thought I was approaching one of the few passing places available and I accelerated in order to get there before this other motorist passed it in the opposite direction – I was convinced that they wouldn't pull in and wait there for me to navigate safely past them; they were just going to ignore it and carry on.

I wasn't sure I would get there in time; I wasn't sure that the passing place was where I remembered it to be. I felt like I was driving too fast myself – *Whatever happens with this other driver*, I thought, *I am driving too fast and there might be black ice.*

When I saw the passing place – just a small grassy verge in front of a five-bar gate – I slammed the brakes on and skidded into it just as the other vehicle rounded the corner not far beyond. The front left of my car just touched the gate and came to a stop less than an inch away from the drystone wall. The other vehicle – I had the impression of something big, a camper van maybe, though all I could see were its headlights – had under-steered ever so slightly, and scraped itself along the wall on the other side of the road. The caterwauling of metal on stone echoed long after the vehicle had disappeared from sight, accompanying the throaty rattle of the fading engine and the strange after-impression I had of laughter, as if somewhere amongst all that commotion I had heard a raucous cackling.

I turned off my own engine, got out of the car and looked up. Round here is one of the best places I know for stargazing. The sky was deep and full, one of those nights where you can look at one tiny bit of sky and the stars just keep appearing for as long as you care to focus.

I stayed there until the noise of the car had faded completely. It took a while; on a clear night in the valley, sound echoes off the mountains for a long time.

While I am driving back to Ravenglass I look over at the sky above Sellafield, where the clouds are livid and turbulent. You can't see Sellafield itself from this route, but Sellafield in the dark is a dramatic sight too: a distant city in a science fiction film . . . a nocturnal city.

I pull into the car park of The Tup, the gravel crunching underneath the tyres. Going out at night is currently the only driving that I do at all, because I don't have to go shopping for food – living and working at here means that I eat here too.

It's about half past three, according to the clock in the car. I turn off the engine and get out. A light drizzle is starting up. I stifle a yawn, and then let it escape.

CHAPTER FIVE

I hear the stairs creaking as I carry the packets of bacon from the big walk-in fridge over to the worktop on the right of the oven.

'Morning, Edie.' Nev pops his big bald head around the kitchen door on his way to the restaurant.

'Morning, Nev,' I say. 'The usual?'

'If you don't mind,' he replies. 'Thanks, pet.'

Nev is a contractor, and he is always first down in the mornings. He has two rashers of bacon, two fried eggs, two sausages, five mushrooms, one bit of fried bread and a small portion of beans. And coffee, of course – they all drink coffee.

I slap his food onto the fryer. When I hear the fat of the bacon hissing, that's when I really wake up. I love the smell of it. And I love feeling that connection with other people up and about so early; it's like we're conspirators of some sort.

Out of the kitchen window I can see the pub's small yard, with grass and weeds growing up through the paving slabs. The caravan's just at the back of the yard, and behind the caravan is the lawn . . . maybe lawn is too grand a word; it's just a bit of grass. There are birds singing, sitting in the trees beyond the grass. I don't know what kind of birds they are; it is something that I've always meant to learn about but have never got around to – one of many such things.

It's slowly getting light and I can hear the stairs creaking again. I break some eggs onto the fryer, whipping my hand away to avoid the hot spitting oil. My hands are covered in burns and scars, but that is something you can't really help in this profession.

Eight o'clock is peak time and there's nobody else on so I'm out there taking orders and in here making the food at the same time, or that's what it feels like at least, being two places at once.

The kitchen is filled with smoke and steam and the smell and sound of half a pig's worth of meat sizzling on the fryer. There are eggs too, and a bit of bread, but it's mostly meat: the contractors like their meat. Meat and coffee.

The extractor fan mounted in the little window tries its best to clear the air, but it's old and clogged with grease, way beyond the point of cleaning. I feel sorry for the thing. The low noise of it sputtering around sounds a lot like the snatches of male voices coming from the restaurant.

So I'm spiking done orders and popping the toaster and filling coffee pots and flipping bacon and taking out loaded plates and nodding morning and taking new orders and then bringing empty plates back in again and it's constant, nonstop, and that's good.

During the week we stop serving breakfasts at nine, so at nine I turn the fryer off and start listening out for the rest of the men departing. After about twenty minutes it sounds like they've all gone, so I go to collect the remaining plates and dishes.

There's a man still sitting at a table. I stand in the doorway, surprised, and look at him. At first he is just a black shape against the window he is sitting in front of, then I can see him properly. He's wearing a black suit and a white shirt.

'Are you okay?' he asks me.

'Yeah!' I say. 'Yeah, sorry – I just– I just thought the room was empty. We stop serving at nine, see.'

'Oh,' he says, standing up, 'I'm sorry.'

'No!' I say. I don't know what I was so shocked by; he's just a man. 'It's fine; I can put the fryer back on. It'll still be hot.'

'Are you sure?'

'I'm sure; it's no problem. Back in a mo.'

I head back into the kitchen, turn the fryer back on and then return to the restaurant and start clearing up the used tables. The man is sitting back down at his window seat.

He is very thin, and has very black hair. He rests his elbows on the table and clasps his hands together in front of his face.

'You a contractor, then?' I ask. 'I don't recognise you.'

'I just got in late last night,' he says, 'but yes, I am a contractor.'

I can't help looking at the clock.

He laughs. 'Don't worry,' he says, 'I'm not running late. I'm going to be doing most of the work from my room. I've got a laptop up there. I'm just staying in the area because I'm involved with a project on site and I've got to be close at hand, just in case. And you know how it is: lots of meetings . . . too many meetings – meetings about meetings.' He rolls his eyes and shakes his head extravagantly.

'Oh,' I say, 'I wouldn't know much about meetings, and nor do I want to. One of many good reasons for working a job like this.'

'Ha,' he says, 'yes, well—'

'What are you having, then?' I ask.

'Coffee,' he replies, quickly, 'please, and bacon, sausages, black pudding.'

'You want any toast?' I ask him. 'Beans, mushrooms, tomatoes, eggs?'

'I suppose I could have some eggs.'

'No problem,' I say, stacking the plates up on my forearms.

'Don't fry the bacon too long,' he says. 'I like it soft.'

'Okay,' I say. 'On its way.'

I go back into the kitchen and put down the dirty crockery, and then set about getting the new contractor some breakfast. Bacon, sausages, black pudding. What kind of person wears a suit when they're working from a pub bedroom? I go back in to the restaurant.

When I take the coffee and the food out to him, he is standing up and looking out of the window. He sits back down once I've put his plate on the table and lays a napkin very carefully over his lap.

'This looks perfect,' he says.

'Good,' I say, though that bacon doesn't look good to me. It's too raw and wet for my tastes. 'Are you with us long, then? Do you want this every morning?'

'I'm here indefinitely,' he says, 'and yes. This every morning would be great. Thank you.'

'It's no problem,' I say.

He just smiles.

'I'll probably see you later,' I say.

Chapter Six

There is a very quiet spell between the post-breakfast clean-up and the early evening. We don't do lunches during the week. The bar is open throughout the day and we leave the door open so that passing walkers know it, but we don't usually get many of them in at once. I usually take the opportunity to turn the music in the kitchen up loud and dance around a bit as I do the prep for the evening meals, and today is no exception.

Maria's doing some paperwork in the bar. In the past she's asked me to leave the door open so she can hear the music, but today she's frowning and her mouth is tight, so I keep the door closed.

I get some pots on the go: a big vegetarian chilli (which is known locally as 'Edie's speciality', but only because nobody else around here really does much in the way of vegetarian food), a lamb casserole, using Herdwick meat, and a beef curry. Then I peel and chop all the vegetables that will accompany the mains – carrots, cabbages, potatoes, that kind of stuff – and I do apples for a big apple pie as well. You have to be doing lots of things at once and you can't stop. That's why it's good to have reggae music on – though it's probably more important when you're in the middle of a rush, because it's easy to get stressed out and lose it a little when you're really busy and the kitchen's really hot.

I wash my hands and go through into the bar to write the specials up on the blackboard, but Maria doesn't look up or say anything. I update the board and then turn to her and ask, 'Are you okay, Maria?'

'I'm okay,' she says. She is leafing through sheets of paper as if she is looking for something.

'Lost something?' I ask.

'No,' she says, and after shuffling them around for a moment longer she puts the papers down. 'It's Gabe. I don't know what to do about him. It is' – she looks at her watch – 'half past one and he is still in bed. He eats rubbish and he eats too much of it. And this morning I had to clean his vomit out of the bathroom sink because he was out all night drinking with his friends again and he was so drunk he could not work out how to be sick in the damned toilet.'

'Why couldn't he do it?'

'He was dead to the world when I went in.'

'Maybe it's just him being a teenager,' I say. 'He's not unkind.'

'He is not unkind, no,' Maria says, 'but he is nineteen! He is old enough to be working, old enough to have a girl-friend. Boys he went to school with are having children by now. Not that he should be doing that, but . . . Gabe just drinks too much, he eats too much, he sleeps too much – he doesn't *do* anything with his time.'

'He does some time behind the bar,' I say. When people are upset about something, I feel compelled to try and make them feel better, even if this means mostly disagreeing with what they're telling me.

'He does not do enough!' Maria snaps. 'And if you think he is so bloody great then next time he is sick all over the bathroom, you clean it up!'

I nod. 'I see what you're saying,' I say. 'Sorry.'

'No,' Maria says. She puts her hand to the bridge of her nose and shakes her head. 'I'm sorry, Edie. I just worry about him.'

'I know,' I say.

'You're talking about me?' It's Gabe's voice.

There is a silence as Maria and I both look up to see Gabe standing in the doorway at the other end of the bar.

'Hi, Gabe,' I say.

Gabe goes behind the bar and finds a pint glass and fills it with lemonade from the fizz tap. He is not tall, but he is quite bulky; Maria is right, he eats too much junk. His shoulders slope downwards, but that could be because he's always got his hands in his jeans pockets and his jeans are baggy and low-down. He has spots and his greasy dark hair hangs down in front of his face. He is always wearing baggy black hoodies that make him look even paler than he is. Today's hoodie is emblazoned with a big red pentagram.

'Been talking long?' he asks.

'No,' Maria says.

'What were you saying?' he asks.

'I was just telling Edie what I found in the bathroom this morning.'

He frowns for a moment, and then remembers. 'Oh yeah,' he says. He smiles lopsidedly. 'Sorry about that. Still don't feel very good.'

Maria turns to me. 'See?' she says. 'No shame.'

'Shame?' Gabe exclaims. 'It's only a bit of sick, Mum.'

'It's *disgusting*,' Maria says.

'It's normal! It's natural! Everybody's sick now and again—'

'You shouldn't get so drunk all the time – and I want you to stop smoking.'

Gabe throws his hands up and opens his mouth. He stands like that for a moment and then points at me. 'Edie smokes!' he says, loudly.

Maria looks at me and I look at her. I do smoke, it's true, though not heavily. Maria knows about it but I still feel bad.

'Edie works for her money. She can do what she wants with it,' Maria says.

'Oh, that's always it with you,' Gabe says. '"Get a job" – like if I get a job I will suddenly be this brilliant person who won't piss you off or something. A son you can be proud of.'

'You're still drunk,' Maria says, 'or hung over. We'll talk about this when you're sober.'

'I don't need to talk about this at all,' Gabe says. 'I'm very content, thank you.'

'As long as you're content, eh?' Maria yells, standing up. 'As long as you're content, everything's fine! That's just it, Gabe – that's how you think!'

I don't think Gabe knows what to say in response. He does look hung-over still; bleary-eyed and unsteady.

'You just do what you want to do! You don't care about me! You don't care about anybody else! You just eat and sleep and smoke and play those silly games!'

'Well, what do you want me to do, Mum?' Gabe says. 'Get a job, right? Where? Where in this shithole can I get a job? Is there a pile of available jobs out there on the beach, just hanging around and waiting for me? Should I just go and pick one?' His voice is getting louder. 'You were the one who brought me to this place, this was your great idea! The only work round here is summer jobs in pubs! And – oh yeah, there's Sellafield; maybe I can join the queue to work at Sellafield and then in ten years or something I can be a fucking teaboy!'

Maria sits back down and folds up. There are things she could say: she could say, *what about university?* Or, *why don't you save up and get a car?* But I know that Maria won't say those things. She is too soft on him. I look at her and she is spent, deflated, like a burst balloon.

Gabe turns slowly, and heads back out of the bar. I hear him ascend the stairs to the living quarters.

'Do you want to talk about it?' I ask Maria.

She shakes her head and, once I know she's sure, I go back through to the kitchen. I turn the reggae down when I get there.

Phillip sidles in at six o'clock every day of the week for his tea. Whenever I think of Phillip I think 'creature of habit' – partly because he is so habitual, and partly because he is such a creature.

He passes from my line of sight and sits at the bar, just as he always does. I have seen him there so many times that I can picture his face and posture exactly. He will still be out there later, after I've finished work. He clears his throat loudly. He does that every day, too.

A moment or two later, Maria comes through with his order.

'Sausage,' I say, quietly, before looking at it. 'Cumberland sausage, peas, mash, fried onions and gravy.'

'You know it,' she says. 'Every bloody night.'

'You told him about the specials?'

'I told him. Don't take it personally, Edie.'

'Oh,' I say, 'I don't. And I wouldn't have expected him to change his order. I just don't understand him.'

'No,' Maria shakes her head. 'Bloody Phillip.'

'Cumberland sausage,' I say, turning to the oven, 'coming up.'

Maria does not really engage any customers in conversation for the rest of the evening. At first she moves quietly away from people after giving them back their change, pretending to have business to attend to further down the bar or beneath the counter, but it is a Friday night and as it gets darker outside the place fills up and Maria does not have to pretend to be busy; there is always somebody waiting.

Maria smiles, the first genuine smile I've seen from her today, when John Senior appears. 'John!' she says.

'Maria,' John says, smiling back. 'Lemonade, please.'

'You back on the soft drinks, then?'

'Aye, thanks.'

Maria moves to the fizz tap. I'm sitting at the end of the bar; John is to my left. To John's left, Phillip Banks sits with his elbows resting on a dry beer towel. He leans against the thick dark upright wooden beam on his left. His hands are clasped together against his cheek, squashed between his head and the beam, the long pale fingers entwined unnaturally. He's looking at John with an almost puzzled expression.

John doesn't look at him until Phillip speaks. 'All right, John?' he says.

John turns his head just enough to make eye-contact and says, 'Right, lad.' Then he turns to face me. 'What's up?' he asks, nodding at Maria. 'Seems stressed?'

'She had a to-do with Gabe,' I whisper, but Maria is back before I can elaborate.

John raises his glass to Maria in thanks, and then drinks. She smiles and wipes the condensation from the glass off her hands.

There's not much of my pint left in the glass. I finish it and start to wonder if the tension I've been aware of all day is lifting.

'Well, I'll tell you what I think Gabe's problem is,' Phillip says, loudly, prompted by nothing obvious.

Maria just looks at him. 'I don't think we were talking about Gabe,' she says.

John looks at me sideways and I can feel myself shrinking.

Phillip looks confusedly from Maria to me and back again. He is good at this mock-confusion thing. 'Edie was just telling us that you've had a row with him,' he says, 'weren't you, Edie?' And then, after a moment's silence, 'It's not a secret, is it?'

Phillip Banks is such a disingenuous fuckwit. One of these days I'm going to stuff his Cumberland sausage full of wasabi paste. Or, better still, thorns from the rosebush out the back.

'I was just explaining to John that you've had a rough day,' I say to Maria.

John says, 'Aye. I were asking.'

Maria shifts her weight from one foot to the other, arms crossed. She looks at me. Her expression is indecipherable.

'Edie didn't say owt about it,' John says. 'It were nowt.'

Then Maria lets loose a great big sigh and slaps her hands down on to the bar top. 'No,' she says, 'no, don't worry. Edie's right, yeah, we had a row. Yes, I'm tired. I'm sorry.'

I sneak a glance at Phillip, who looks slightly disappointed. It's now ten o'clock so he's been here for four hours, drinking quite solidly. Everything about him has gone sloppy.

I go round the bar to pull myself another pint while Maria tells John – and Phillip, though only because he happens to be there – what she told me earlier, and then about the argument that she had with Gabe. Phillip keeps opening his mouth as if to speak, and eventually, Maria gives him the opportunity.

'Those louts are a disgrace,' Phillip says, 'playing those horrible games, or else roaming the streets with their hoods up.'

There is a silence.

'Which louts?' Maria asks. 'Were we talking about louts?'

'Your— The lads round here,' Phillip says with a wave of his hand, 'always on the bloody bench. The ones your Gabe hangs around with – you know the crowd. They all need to grow up a bit, start living in the real world instead of playing those stupid games and taking drugs. I can smell the smoke from their cigarettes – and they're not cigarettes' – he leans forwards over the bar and stage-whispers – 'if you know what I mean.'

'My son is not a lout,' Maria says, leaning into Phillip's face. 'Now you get out. I've had enough of you for one night.'

Phillip splutters and looks around. 'I just meant he's fallen in with the wrong crowd.'

'Only crowd round here,' John mutters.

'He's not with his own kind, is he?' Phillip continues, ignoring John. 'Must be hard for him.'

'What do you mean, his own kind?' Maria demands. Her hands are on her hips now.

'Y'know,' Phillip says, but nobody helps him out and eventually he looks down and sighs. 'Polish people,' he says.

John and I look at each other. It's almost hard not to laugh. Maria just points to the door and Phillip clumsily removes himself from the bar stool and shrugs his coat on. 'See you tomorrow,' he says.

Nobody replies. None of us speaks at all until he's gone.

'Been a while since he made that mistake,' I say.

'Three weeks,' Maria says. 'Longest stretch yet. Thought he'd learned how to hold his tongue.'

John asks for another lemonade and Maria pours him one.

'Normally I can just ignore his nonsense,' she says, passing the glass over, 'but not tonight.'

'You're too good to him anyways,' John says. 'I wouldn't have him back at all.'

'Like I say,' Maria says, 'normally I can just ignore it.'

'Gabe can always come help on the farm,' John says, 'though we can't pay much.'

Maria acknowledges this with a brief smile, but doesn't say anything.

'How's John?' I ask.

'He's all right,' John says. 'Quiet, but then, he's always been quiet.' He looks sideways at me. 'He likes you, y'know. Won't do anything about it, but he does.'

I go hot and Maria laughs.

'I don't like him,' I say. 'I mean, I— Not like that. Oh God, I'm sorry. That came out wrong. I mean—'

'Don't worry,' John says, looking down, 'I understand.'

'I haven't seen him since Greycroft,' I say.

'No,' John says, 'he's been under the weather.' He finishes his drink and places the empty glass on the bar. 'Right. I'm off. Nice to see you both again. Shame about Phillip, but there's always one.'

He grips my shoulder as a goodbye gesture and his fingers feel like iron pincers. 'Bye,' he says, and he waves at Maria on the other side of the bar and then he leaves.

Chapter Seven

I check my emails and find a Facebook friend request from Phillip Banks – another Phillip Banks, maybe? It can't be the Phillip Banks we all know and love, surely. He wouldn't lower himself to joining something like Facebook? He's been pretty vocal about it before: 'a load of pimply layabouts swapping guff' was what I think he said.

I click through to look at the profile. It is him, after all. I sit back. Maybe he's learned that lots of users are closer to his age than mine. He'll probably end up part of some network of pervy old men or confused, vitriolic right-wingers and love it.

I let the cursor hover over the 'Accept' button, and then I press it. Curiosity, I suppose. And because I can't be bothered trying to explain to him why I've ignored the request. Then – and I know I shouldn't, I know it'll annoy me – I start to browse his Wall.

'hmm whats this then'

'hmm is this it then the great and mighty facebook haha'

'hello friends!'

'hmm arent any of you at work or anything'

'what is lol is it lots of love or is it a man drowning'

'Does grammar not matter here!!!'

On and on it goes. He hasn't got many Facebook friends yet and so there aren't any comments. A couple of 'likes' but then people will 'like' anything. The only thing on his Wall that is not some inane, vaguely superior status update is a link, with an accompanying note:

'hmm this makes for very intresting reading very thought provoking indeed, glad somebody is not afraid to say what they think lol'

He must have Googled 'lol', then. Unless he means 'lots of love'. Though that's not something I can imagine him ever saying.

I do some reading about the Greycroft stone circle, and then – against my better judgement – navigate back to Phillip's profile page and click on the link. It takes me to a blog called 'This Green and Pleasant Land'.

Well well well, what have we here. I have woken up in the year 2150 and let me tell you, GREAT Britain is very different indeed! It's not so GREAT any more!

After decades of consecutive centre-left governments and their virtually open-door approach to border controls, our once-pretty little island is looking quite full. Oh, what happened to our Avalon? Our early morning mists, our green rolling hills? The fields are being concreted over, the forests are being steam-rollered. Because Britain is FULL. Full to BURSTING!!!! Full of people looking for a safe haven, people looking for the land of plenty. And we've got to build more houses! The cites are growing like fungus, sprouting upwards and outwards. Grey towers rising into the sky. Car parks and motorways and rows of dingy little box-homes replacing moorland and greenbelt. Imagine those photos of cities in Japan – well that's what GREAT Britain looks like now, but all over with no space in between! Can you believe it! Neon lights everywhere and strip clubs full of Eastern Europeans gyrating their diseased crotches in young men's faces, yes, corrupting them in more ways than one. Islamic terrorists preaching hatred and intolerance from their bulbous mosques. Romanian women sending their dirty little children out to beg. African refugees fleeing tribal blood feuds, their faces striped with scars.

Jamaican Yardies speeding through crowded streets waving their guns out of the windows. Hands in the air like they just don't care! There's no proper music any more, just Bollywood shit and that jungle music that once upon a time - back at the turn of the millennium - only black gangsters listened to. Or should that be 'gangstas'? Yes, even our language has changed. Our English language, the tongue that shaped the world, is being perverted by ethnic youth 'culture'. Properly spoken or written Queen's English is rarely witnessed any more, as is - dare I say it - the white skin of this country's natives. As successive generations have become less and less respectful of tradition and their heritage, interracial relationships have become more and more common, until we've reached the current sad state of affairs - a universally muddy skin colour, meaning you can hardly discern people's genealogy any more! Not that the descendants of true Brits are anything to be proud of these days. They're uncouth, half-naked, promiscuous, homosexual, work-shy, crusty mollycoddled statists who don't know left from right from wrong or their arses from their mouths. Is this what our ancestors fought for in the great wars of the twentieth century? That dim and distant past when men were men and women women looks so rosy now.

Haha, of course I have not really travelled into the

future. What I am presenting to you is what the future will look like if things carry on unchecked! The bleeding-heart lefties and the PC brigade would have you believe that this is just a fantasy, that there is no reason to call out the less savoury aspects of our foreign friends. Or, even better, that these less savoury aspects do not exist! They say that people from faraway countries need our help, they need 'asylum'. And they're 'not that bad'. Well, I've got news for you, folks, this country is only great because of US! The people who were born of it, the people who died for it, the generations of hard-working indigenous citizens with good moral compasses and fundamentally superior values. That's right, I said it. SUPERIOR. And by coming here and swamping us with their different cultures, these immigrants are ruining it! Instead of being inspired by us, they're stealing what we've made! Maybe a minuscule proportion of them really do need asylum, I don't know, but the point is that they've made their countries the messes that they are and they can't just run around the world looking for places where the grass is greener. LOOK AFTER YOUR OWN BLOODY GRASS!

I have seen the future, and in it our lovely land has been overrun by scum and by foreigners. Our rural idyll, our woodland walks and babbling brooks, our cricket pitches and thatched cottages, our lofty peaks and hidden valleys, our unspoilt beaches and our seaside humour, our little country pubs, everything we hold dear – all of it gone, swept away by a tsunami of illegal immigrants and boundless breeding, all of it buried beneath an endless concrete splurge built to house those who were once our enemies. IS THIS RIGHT?! No of course it isn't, and any right-minded person can see that. We need to act now, we need to tell our MPs and our media that ENOUGH IS ENOUGH!!! We need a good strong leader who is not afraid to FIX THE HOLES IN THE FENCE. We need a new CHURCHILL. We need a NEW KING ARTHUR. In the legends we are told that King Arthur will rise again when England needs him most. WELL ENGLAND NEEDS HIM NOW!!!!!!!!!

Hmm, indeed. Makes you think, does it, Phillip? You idiot.

The rain is easing off and the clouds are parting to reveal a pale-blue sky beyond. I open the caravan door and light another cigarette. I check the time on my phone.

After I've finished the cigarette, I put on my trainers and coat and leave the caravan. I get in the car and drive away from The Tup.

The walk to Greycroft seems half the distance this time – not because I'm on my own, but because I know where I'm going, and I don't get distracted by Newton Manor either, or at least not a lot; I stop and look at the broken top-floor windows – they are cold and black and deep – but then I carry on walking. I feel much more certain than I did last time that there is something in there, behind those windows.

My walk breaks into a jog.

By the time I get to Greycroft the sky is mostly blue and the clouds are mostly white. The stones are dry to the touch, but the grass is still wet. I should've brought my cagoule to sit on. The sea looks choppy, with odd white foam tops appearing and disappearing all over. And Sellafield looks like it always does.

I remember standing in a field much like this, but on the far side, watching from a distance as the cooling towers were demolished. They were huge structures and I'd loved them for as long as I'd lived in the area. They looked so majestic as you drove along the A595 and watched the sun set into the sea behind them, their smooth, concave sides sharply silhouetted against the fiery sky. I once went to Sellafield Visitors' Centre with my parents when I was little and we went on a tour of the site. The little bus took us right past the base of the cooling towers, which were open at the bottom so you could look right up inside them. Water cascaded down the interior, not a waterfall but like rain during a monsoon – never-ending rain. I'd wanted to climb inside and just lie there looking up.

When the cooling towers came down there were crowds of people all over the countryside with binoculars and video cameras, some celebrating, some sad. The news crews had the best spots. It was a sunny day, I think, or at least it was dry. I was there with Maria and Gabe and we sat on a blanket and ate Scotch eggs and drank orange juice. We watched and watched and then, all of a sudden a cloud of dust erupted from the base of one of the towers and it slowly collapsed, not like something made out of brick but like a curtain coming down: something gentle and soft. There was no sound at first; the waves reached us more or less as the top of the tower fell into the dust and out of sight, just a long, low rumble.

I don't know what I was expecting, but something louder, more of a sense of destruction, on a par with the scale of the towers themselves; they deserved that. They deserved a loud noise, an explosion.

Tears pricked my eyes as the last one fell.

I wish I could lie down inside a cooling tower now and look up at a small circle of sky as water poured down all around me. I lie down in the middle of the stone circle instead, despite the wet grass. What are our stone circles? What do we build that will last as long as this? What will be as iconic or mysterious in thousands of years? Cooling towers maybe, if there are any left.

I close my eyes and listen to the seagulls. My heartbeat

sounds like Gabe running up and down the stairs at The Tup, which he does sometimes as an attempt at exercise. The sense of *up-and-down* is very real; I feel like my heart sinks towards my stomach and then rises up towards my gullet as I try to control it and then lose control of it, in a repeating pattern. I open my eyes again.

The internet told me that Greycroft stone circle is Bronze Age: four thousand five hundred years old. It was buried by the farmer who owned the land in 1820, because it was in the way, and then excavated by one of his successors in 1949. At the time of excavation they found a cairn in the middle of it which is believed to mark the spot of an ancient cremation. Whether the cairn was found as a result of the circle being excavated or the circle was excavated as a result of the cairn being found, I'm not sure. Either way, I'm lying in that very spot right now.

The Candle said its remains were here. It said its body had been burned. But I can't feel its presence. Maybe that's what I felt at Newton Manor.

I become aware of a very low, quiet humming: a drone that sounds almost vocal. It doesn't have the high, buzzy quality of electricity wires; it is something else.

For a split-second after I open my eyes I indulge the impression that the stones have been crowding around me, looking down, and are suddenly hurrying back to their rightful places. Lying flat on my back, looking up at the sky, I am still aware of them just touching my peripheral vision; their points are visible enough to give the sky above a circular edge.

As I get to my feet I realise how cold and wet my back is. I look around, though I don't know what for. I set off walking around the circle, running my hand over the top of each stone as I pass it. Nothing happens. I don't know what I want to happen.

As long as I'm here at Greycroft, I feel like I'm waiting for something.

PART TWO

. . . the lake in a previous letter. But we also used to go swimming in the rivers. There was one that was our favourite, down at the bottom of Eskdale. It was a bit of a walk to get there – probably why we had it to ourselves so often. But like letting yourself get hungry before a good meal, the walk was part of the pleasure.

You had to hurry through this farmyard without being seen – the old farmer there was forever chasing people away – and hit out, up the fellside, following the river. There was a dusty path to follow, mostly used by sheep I think – those tough old Herdwicks – which wound uphill, on and on. My memories of this place are coloured by the weather. The way I remember it, it was always baking hot, the earth hard and dry, the sky clear of all clouds and a deep blue.

We'd walk past stretches of river that were perfectly serviceable, really, and often we'd spy other swimmers who had settled for these lower pools. But we knew the spot we wanted.

When you got up high enough, there was a long, deep passage where the water was turquoise and smooth old rocks that had soaked up the sun's rays were hot like radiators, perfect for drying towels.

This pool was book-ended by two smaller, shallower pools, in which the water swirled around and around. You could slide down a waterfall which connected them, shooting from one to the other. Being up there, Edith, having such a joyful, secret location to yourself — you feel separate from the world, apart from it, as if you are in your own place, a place that exists only for you.

On one side of the pool the rocks provided a little cliff, and we would dare each other to jump off of it. For the very brave, there was one gnarled old tree that grew from the top of this cliff — I'd climb that tree myself occasionally, usually only if there was a new girl to impress. Though of course none of those girls came close to you in spirit or appearance, Edith. If only I'd known about you back then . . .

CHAPTER EIGHT

John has become this man in my mind who never moves from one spot; whenever I see him or imagine him, he's sat there in his seat, lit by the firelight, looking deeply wrinkled.

'It's good of you to keep on coming round now, Edie,' he says. 'Since Girt's gone, I've felt lonely an' old. It's good to have someone to talk to.'

'No problem,' I say, 'I like seeing you.'

'I wish me damn son would be a bit more hospitable, like, but you can't control folk, I s'pose.'

'You certainly can't.'

'I miss her, Edie, now more than ever.'

'Girt?'

'Christina.'

'Oh, sorry.'

'Seems like I've gone into a dark world, all of a sudden,

like – like things have changed, just now, the past few days or weeks. I'm losing track of time, for one thing, an' I can't face the farm like I used to.'

'Maybe that's just getting old,' I say.

He looks at me sharply, and then his face softens. 'Aye,' he says, 'you're probably right.'

'I miss my grandparents very much,' I say. 'I miss everything about them. And I can't imagine what it must be like losing your true love. What I saw my grandma go through . . . She was older than you, but still. I couldn't go through it myself.'

He nods slowly, pursing his lips. 'It's tough, all right,' he says.

'What about Christina do you miss the most?' I ask.

He thinks for a long time, and thinks and thinks, and gradually his eyes fill up a bit, and I think he's forgotten that I asked a question. I don't want to remind him, though.

The thing is that I do not understand, not really, how anybody can get wrapped up in a relationship without thinking about the inevitable end of it. It's a horrible but unavoidable truth that the best, happiest relationships will end in absolutely the worst and most painful way. Maybe though, overall, the happiness you get throughout your life kind of balances out the vicious stabbing of bereavement in the end. Maybe. That must be the case, otherwise people wouldn't do what they do to themselves.

Sometimes I think I should be in a relationship, or perhaps

I should try to find someone that I could fall in love with, even just a little bit, enough to see what it's like – dip a toe in the water, as it were. I probably could if I put my mind to it, but when I do think seriously about it, I get almost unbearably sad and scared and I have very violent dreams where I'm killing people, people I care about, like Grandma and Granddad and Maria. Nothing else upsets me as much as worrying that maybe I do want a relationship after all. I'm very lucky and unusual in that I can decide against that, I think. I can feel scared and have the bad dreams and then wake up and think, no, it's okay, let's not worry about it. I don't want a relationship after all. It's almost as if I'm choosing what kind of human to be, as opposed to it being predetermined, which is how it seems to be for most people. I can very easily choose to feel very little, is what I'm trying to say, and that is a far more comfortable way to live than feeling a lot. I think some-times I feel like an animal – or more accurately, a plant, or maybe even more accurately, a stone. I still think I would like to be a stone.

I finish the glass of sloe gin that John gave me, and refill it from the sticky bottle that's on the floor.

The truth is, now I'm on the subject, that what Grandma used to tell me about stone circles – that the stones in a stone circle were girls who danced too long – resonates with me in a truly powerful way, in the sense that I feel it vibrating inside my head. Sometimes I think that maybe it

chimes so totally with something inside me that the resonance works itself up into a state where it accentuates itself,
tearing apart the fabric of me. Resonance disaster, that's
called; where something mechanical or structural starts to
resonate, and then ends up swaying violently, so violently
that it breaks up.

I wonder what it felt like for those girls as they were
turned into stones. Did they feel relieved to have stopped
dancing? To have a rest? To stop thinking and worrying and
feeling at all?

I finish the second glass of sloe gin too and John has still
not answered my question – or spoken at all, in fact, since
I asked it. I stand up and leave the room, and I'm not sure
that he sees me go.

Mrs Cook is one of our semi-regulars. She comes in about
once a week for a drink and a catch-up. She would probably come in more frequently but she doesn't walk around
very much – walking is difficult for her because she's so
big. There's not really a better way to put it. She pants her
way to The Tup, her long dress floating around her so that
she looks like a jellyfish, and she is so exhausted by the
time she arrives that she can't even speak for about fifteen
minutes.

I'm sitting at a table with Mrs Cook, Phillip, John Senior
and a new contractor called Jason. Above the table is a big
glass case on the wall in which a stuffed fox prowls for ever.

Maria is having an actual rest, upstairs; Gabe is doing one of his rare turns behind the bar.

'It's just unbelievable,' gasps Mrs Cook, not for the first time. 'Why would anybody do such a thing? Who could?' She is one of those people who feels things very intensely, so she has been crying on and off since she heard about Girt. She shakes her head.

'You know who could do such a thing,' Phillip whispers loudly. 'That bloody Gabe, that's who; Gabe and his mob of delinquents, slouching around in their Satanist hoodies and smoking their cannabis.' He's emphasising certain words as a result of trying not to speak too loudly. I haven't seen him this excited since Derrick Bird did his thing.

'It's a promising introduction to the area,' Jason says. 'My first day and it's all talk of animal mutilation.' He laughs and drinks half his pint in one go. He is big – not at all fat, just really big – and covered in tattoos. He's already asked us to call him Pitbull.

'Don't joke about it, Jason,' Mrs Cook says. 'Some things shouldn't be joked about!'

'It's Pitbull,' says Pitbull, 'and yeah, okay, I'm sorry: I just joke about more or less everything, I guess. It's in my nature.' He downs the rest of his pint. 'Good beer,' he says, and stands up. 'Anyone for another?'

Phillip eyes him distastefully while he's at the bar. 'What kind of man would call himself Pitbull?' he asks. 'And what kind of man would let himself get so fat? He'll regret all those tattoos one day, when all that extra skin goes wrinkly. If he even lives long enough to get old, what with all that weight. It's disgusting. And those tattoos are disgusting – all them naked women. He's disgusting all over.' He slurps from his glass. 'There's no hope for people,' he says. 'No hope at all.'

John and I look at each other and John shakes his head. Phillip doesn't notice. He's looking back at Pitbull.

'Jason's not fat,' Mrs Cook says, quietly.

'I think it's mostly muscle,' I say. 'You don't want to let him overhear you talking like that, Phillip. He might not take too kindly to it. He might beat you up.'

'Give you a good hiding,' John adds.

'Aye, well,' Phillip says.

'So why do you think Gabe killed Girt?' I ask. 'It seems a bit extreme.'

''s nonsense,' John murmurs.

'You know who it was, then, eh, John?' Phillip demands.

'Naw,' John says, 'but it sure as sheepshit weren't Gabe. He's not a bad lad.'

'How do you know that?'

'Why would it be Gabe?' John says.

'Who else would it be? Him and his weird friends are always wearing hoodies with pictures of blood and symbols all over them, and listening to that heavy metal music. Not to mention the games – those video games. Have you seen how violent they are? They're always on the news.' He leans forwards and puts both his hands palm down on the table. 'Those games teach people to enjoy killing,' he pronounces, proudly. Then he lifts his hands and sits back. 'Plus,' he says, 'they all take drugs. So . . . y'know. I'm not claiming to know for sure, of course I can't know for sure, but I think it's clear which way everything points.'

'Aye,' John says, 'everything points to bullshit.'

'You'll be eating your words before long,' Phillip says. 'Trust me: if it wasn't that gang of reprobates, then who was it?'

'I can't say I know,' John says, 'and so I won't.'

'Do you actually know Gabe at all, Phillip?' I ask.

'No more than I want to,' Phillip says, and sniffs. His eyes dart around the bar. 'Where's Maria tonight, anyway?'

'Having a well-deserved rest,' I say. 'Why?'

'No reason,' Phillip answers, his eyes briefly meeting mine and then darting away again.

Pitbull sits back down, placing a number of pints on the table. 'What did I miss?' he says.

'Phillip's theories about Gabe,' I say.

'I see,' Pitbull says. He laughs again; a big laugh, a nice laugh. 'Next you'll be saying I did it because I'm new around here.'

John snorts and Phillip looks put out. After a moment, he leans over the table towards Pitbull and asks, 'Why have you got so many tattoos?'

Pitbull leans in as well, his face hardening. He stares at

Phillip and then answers the question. 'One for every kid I've killed,' he whispers.

Phillip looks confused. He continues to look confused, even after Pitbull has burst out laughing, even when Mrs Cook joins in with a nervous little giggle.

Even when I explain, 'It's a joke! He hasn't really killed any kids!'

But Phillip just glares at me, at everyone. 'You all think you're so clever,' he says, once it's quiet enough, 'so bloody clever and open-minded and everything. But you're blind. You're ignorant. You're naïve. And you'll regret it.'

'Listen,' John says, 'I've got no time for you, Phillip. Never have and never will. But I hold my tongue because as far as I'm concerned you can say and do whatever the hell you like. But the truth is you're a bigot. We don't jump to the same conclusions as you every time we see a tattoo or a hoodie, not because we're blind, but because we're decent. There might not be any hope for people, mebbe you're right about that. But it's not because of folk like Gabe or Pitbull here; it's because of folk like you. Now git.'

He lifts up a walking stick from beneath the table and pokes Phillip in the shoulder with it. 'Git,' he repeats.

'Are you asking me to move?' Phillip says.

'Tellin',' says John.

Phillip scowls and scrapes his chair noisily along the floor. John stands up and moves out from behind the table. He's a bit unsteady; he's been drinking again.

'See you soon,' he says.

As John leaves, somebody else ducks into the pub.

'Jesus Christ,' Phillip mutters. 'So many strangers at the same time.'

'You mean two,' I say.

The man approaches the bar and talks to Gabe. He is wearing a modern waterproof coat, walking boots, brown cords, and thick glasses with a bright-green cord to keep them on his head. Gabe points in our direction and the man turns around. He grins at us and heads over. The glasses magnify his eyes, and coupled with the fact that his grin doesn't disappear, the effect is to make him look manically happy. He has curly, greying hair.

'Now then,' he says, with a faint Devonshire accent, 'which one of you two gents is Phillip Banks?'

'That'd be me,' Phillip says.

The man holds out his hand. 'We spoke on the phone,' he says. 'Keith Mason. From the paper.'

'Oh,' Phillip says. 'I didn't think that – um . . .' He falls silent and then lifts his hands up and shakes his head slightly.

'What?' asks the man from the paper. His voice is a bit phlegmy, a bit wet. He sounds like he coughs a lot. He also doesn't really finish his words properly – I don't mean he drops the final letter; it's like he never closes his mouth so all of his words run together. He has big square yellow teeth.

'I didn't think that . . .' Phillip trails off again.

'What?' says the man, again. He is smiling, as if everything is funny. I don't understand what's going on. I say 'smiling', but maybe that's not right. He's got a mouth like a dinosaur's mouth.

'Has Phillip contacted you about something?' asks Mrs Cook.

'Yes,' says the man. Keith. I look at Phillip, and Philip's looking at Keith and shaking his head.

'Wait,' I say, and grin at Phillip, 'I've got it: Phillip contacted you about something, but he didn't want anybody else to know about it – right? Is that it, Phillip?'

Phillip's face is white and his mouth slack. He looks at me for a moment and then says, 'No – no! Just— Keith, just let me get up and get you a drink.' He stands and in doing so knocks the table with his knees and all of the drinks slop over the edge of their glasses. Phillip wobbles and nearly falls back down. His face is turning red again, so red I feel like I can see it swelling up with blood. He mutters a 'fucking hell' and then manages to extricate himself, and by the time he's finally standing up straight he's flustered and embarrassed and uncomfortable and it's brilliant.

Keith looks around at everybody with his massive magnified eyes and laughs. His laugh is a comic-book *yakyakyak*.

The two of them turn and head over to the bar, Keith still laughing.

*   *   *

I suspected that Keith Mason would be staying here with us and, sure enough, he's sitting in the dining room when I go through to take orders in the morning.

'Coffee, please,' he says, smiling. He looks up at me over the top of his glasses. 'Black. And scrambled eggs – but a big one, a large portion, if that's possible? I don't mean to be any trouble but if it's okay, four eggs?'

'No problem,' I say, making a note on the pad. All around us, other guests are looking up from their food. I don't think it's his order that's drawing attention, he's just got a loud voice. 'Brown toast or white?'

'Ooh, white,' he says. 'And don't toast it too long. Leave it pale and interesting.' He laughs at himself then, and smiles his dinosaur smile. For fuck's sake: so many people think 'pale and interesting' is an interesting thing to say about toast.

'No problem,' I say.

'Give us a smile,' he says.

I look at him. He doesn't make me want to smile. I don't smile.

He winks, not in a salacious way, but it's still over-familiar, over-friendly. I remain unsmiling.

I take the orders from the other guests. Pitbull is there and he raises his eyebrows and nods in Keith's direction as I approach him. I shake my head and roll my eyes. Pitbull laughs, a small, silent laugh, and that's okay. That's nice.

Pitbull's all right. Though I do wish sometimes that more women would stay in this place.

I don't do anything horrible to Keith's scrambled eggs. I don't ever do anything horrible to anybody's food, however tempting it is sometimes. I just look at that mound of egg quivering there and pull a face, an expression of disgust. I stick my tongue out and mime being sick, then I look out of the greasy window at the rain and then I pick up Keith's plate and a couple of the plates for other guests and I take them through.

'He's been asking us loads of questions,' says Maria from behind the laptop. I sit opposite her and drink my orange juice. The pub is gloomy with brown light in the way only pubs during the day can be. 'Loads of questions about me and Gabe, and about the Platts. About Girt – that's what he's here for, something to do with Girt.'

'He's a creep,' I say.

'He's okay,' Maria says, 'but he wants something and I don't know what it is.'

'Yeah,' I say, 'sounds like a creep. Him and bloody Phillip: they're up to something.'

Maria nods, but she doesn't look away from the laptop – she never looks away from the laptop as long as it's open. 'Bloody Phillip,' she says. 'I agree with you there. He is the worrying thing. Perturbing. He is the perturbing thing.'

I finish the orange juice and stand. 'I'll let you do your books,' I say. 'I'll be back in for the teas.'

'The dinners.'

'Yeah, the dinners. Whatever, Trevor.'

Maria still doesn't look up but she is smiling, I can tell.

Of course Keith is there in the bar later, when I come through from the kitchen after finishing the teas. The *dinners*. Keith, Phillip and Maria.

'Hello there,' Keith says, grinning. The words come out as a slow *ellother*, shaped by his smile, by his teeth. 'Can I get you a drink?'

'No thanks,' I say, without meeting his eyes. 'I get them free because I work here.'

As I move behind the bar and get myself a pint, he gets off his bar stool and repositions it so that it's on the other side of mine, so that I'm between him and Phillip.

I look at him. 'What are you doing?' I ask.

'I'm just making it easier for us to talk.'

'What do you mean?'

'I just want to ask you a few questions.' He gets a small silver digital recorder out of his coat pocket and puts it on the top of the bar.

'Seriously,' I say, and I can't keep the laugh from my voice, 'what the fuck do you think you're doing?'

'I just want to record our conversation,' he says. 'I'm writing a piece for the paper.'

'Which paper do you write for?' I ask.

'I'm freelance,' he says.

'Well, which paper is this piece for, then?'

'Don't worry!' he says, and he laughs that laugh. His mouth doesn't open much when he laughs; it just stays in its smile shape. 'I'm not going to stitch anybody up!'

He's either intentionally avoiding the question or he's an idiot. The former, probably.

'What's it about?' I ask.

'Animal mutilation,' he says, and he blinks at me.

Girt. I could tell him where to go – which would be my preference – but I could probably do more good by talking to him. I put my hands flat on the top of the bar and nod. 'All right then,' I say, 'turn on your machine and ask away.'

Keith presses a button on the digital recorder and a small red light appears. 'Okay,' he says, 'I'm in The Tup with Edie, who works in the kitchen. What's your surname, Edie?'

'I'm the chef.'

'I'm sorry?'

'I said, I'm the chef. You said that I work in the kitchen, and I'm telling you that I'm the actual chef.'

'Okay then. Okay then. So, what's your surname?'

'Grace,' I say. I'm regretting this already.

'Edie Grace. And how long have you lived in the area?'

'Seven years. Since I was eighteen.'

'Where have you stayed since arriving?'

'Here.' I point behind me to the kitchen. 'In a caravan out back.'

'You've been living in a caravan for seven years?' Keith's smile is back.

'Yep.'

'And have you been happy here?'

'Yes, very.'

'You must get lonely, though.'

'Not at all.'

'Or bored?'

'Is this relevant? I thought you were supposed to be asking about animal mutilation.'

'I need to get a feel for the people and the place,' Keith says. 'I'm not just going to write a list of facts about the dog – that wouldn't work as a feature, would it? But don't worry, I'm not going to stitch you up.'

'You don't have to keep saying that,' I say.

Keith laughs again. 'Do you get bored, then?' he asks.

'No,' I say, 'I like it here. That's why I'm here, and not somewhere else.'

'You have no ambition to buy your own place one day? Your own house, your own property?'

'No,' I say, leaning in. 'Look, I'm not sure how much I want to tell you about myself. If all you're going to do is judge me and disparage my whole bloody life then you can fuck right off.'

'Okay, okay,' Keith says, and he holds his hands up in front of him and raises his eyebrows. 'No affront intended, I assure you. I'll ask about something else. How long have you known Maria and Gabe?'

'As long as I've lived here.'

'And did you ever know Gabe's father?'

'No.'

'It must have been hard for Gabe, growing up here. He didn't choose it like you did.'

'I don't know. He has friends; it's a good place in a lot of ways.'

'Good for some, sure, but a teenage boy? Where do Gabe and his friends go? What do they do for fun?'

'They don't cut up dogs, if that's what you're implying.'

'What?'

'Look,' I say, and I lean into Keith's face. He has thick skin. 'I know Phillip put you on to this, and I know what he'll have told you about Gabe, and it's nonsense. Everything that idiot says is nonsense. You'd do well to disregard it all.' I finish my pint and hop down from the stool. 'Now, I'm not answering any more of your questions. I was going to; I was thinking that my answers would maybe balance out some of Phillip's bile. But these questions of yours are weird. They don't fit. So no, no more questions, no more answers.'

Keith looks at me. He brings his hands back up, palms forwards, protesting innocence. He's still grinning.

'Goodnight, Maria,' I shout, and she turns from serving a customer to wave briefly. I don't say anything to Phillip.

I just—

John Junior is sitting on the scrubby grass with his back against the gnarled stone gatepost that marks Girt's grave, looking out towards the sea. He's been crying, and as I watch he hulks over, puts his hands to his face and rolls so that he's lying on the ground by Girt's grave, shaking with sobs, not unlike his father did the night we buried her. John's clothes are soaking up all the wet from the ground as he lies there, because the ground around here is always wet, isn't it? It's always raining or been raining, or it's morning dew or melting frost or misty. In the distance the sea is cold and grey and rough. John crawls around so that he's kneeling at the foot of Girt's grave and then he bows his head as if to pray. If you didn't know Girt was buried there then actually you wouldn't be able to tell; you'd just wonder at the presence of a gatepost in such a location – I mean, in a place where there was obviously never any fence or gate.

'Edie!' The word is accompanied by a sharp pain across my face. 'Edie!'

'What?' I shake my head. I'm looking at Maria. 'Did you *slap* me?'

'What is wrong? Edie, is there something wrong?'

'What? No. I—' I look around. I'm still in the bar, and

Keith and Phillip are whispering to each other as they look at me curiously. 'I was just remembering something,' I say. 'I mean, it was a memory, or an idea for the future . . . but . . . sorry. I'm tired. It wasn't a memory. It was somebody imagining something. I mean it was me imagining something. I don't know what I mean. I just drifted off or something.'

'You just stopped moving and slumped,' Maria says, 'but your eyes were still open. You looked like a zombie.'

'Yeah,' I say, 'I'm sorry.'

'Don't apologise, you idiot! Get some rest.' She pulls me close and rubs my back like Grandma used to. 'I work you too hard. Now go!'

But I don't go; I keep hold of her and I don't let her let go of me and suddenly I'm sobbing into her neck and her shoulder like a scared child, and she's holding me up, and my stomach and chest are heaving as I cry, and she's shushing me, stroking my hair and my back, whispering Polish endearments into my ear, and rocking me from side to side.

I try to talk several times, but don't manage it. The pub has gone quiet. My crying is deafening, and sounds snotty. I pull Maria towards the kitchen, hoping she understands, and she gets the message and leads me through into the darker, more private space.

'I'm sorry,' I say. 'I don't know what's happening to me, Maria. I'm going mad.'

'You are not going mad,' she says, holding my face and looking into my eyes. Her gaze is stern. 'You are not going mad; it's just the world we live in. This stuff with Girt? It's horrible. And you are tired, Edie. I need to get that son of mine taking some of your shifts. And I will. The next few weeks, you take some nights off, okay? Mitchell and Gabe and I can do it. We won't cook as well as you, but I don't want you getting ill. You're like my daughter, you know that. I care for you.'

I nod.

'Okay? Look at me, Edie.'

I look at her and say, 'Yes, thank you, Maria – so much. I'm okay. It's okay.'

She hugs me again, and this time I keep it together until she has let me go and I have returned to the caravan, where it comes again, the sobbing like a wave, like nightfall.

After a while I wipe the tears from my face. I look around the caravan. It's all fucking shit. It's crap, all of it. I tear all of my pictures down from the walls and open all of the cupboard doors in the kitchenette and slam them closed again, one by one. I take my phone from my pocket and throw it at the ceiling. And *when* was it okay, honestly, when was it okay, really, when was it ever really *okay*? Am I a fuck-up? That's a question I suppress sometimes. I get all of my clothes out and try to rip them to pieces. I want a home to go to. I don't want to live in a fucking caravan for the rest of my life and I don't know what to do about it.

Fucking hell. How *dare* he. How dare Keith say it's boring? What the fuck does he know about me? That leathery fucking dickhead with his digital fucking recorder and his big yellow teeth. I should have hit him. I should have broken his nose. Wherever you go, whatever you do, you end up being pissed off by a fucking tosspot.

And I don't want to think about the future is the point, is where I was going with all this. Him asking me about my life, asking questions he's got no right to ask, and the sad truth is he hit a nerve. I don't know what I'm doing with my life. I don't feel like you should have to know, but you do, or you end up fucked.

I don't want to feel time passing like it does, and it's true, it goes by faster as you get older. And I feel like I waste so much of it. But I don't know what to do that is worthwhile. What makes a difference?

And poor Mags being so ill and poor Don looking after her and watering the fucking Tup plants, day in, day out. He can't even bear to eat his tea in the same house as his sick wife. And then there's John Senior, eternally bereaved, guilty and sad and horny as fuck. I don't want to end up like any of them.

I came here for my reasons and they were good reasons. I wanted to get away; to get away from people. I came here after Grandma died, after I found those letters, because Granddad made it sound so perfect and idyllic and that's what I wanted, I wanted the country, I wanted solitude and simplicity. I wanted to escape. I wanted to be somewhere where time moves more slowly and where death is further away. And there is beauty here in these landscapes, and in the bleakness, and there is time to be found in the valleys and on the shores of the lakes if you're still enough, and when you wait and watch, the mist comes down from the mountains and you can feel peace in a rare and deep way. But I can't live like this for ever. What will happen when I'm old? It's not as if I'm saving for a pension from my Tup wage. I don't think I'll want to be living in a caravan when I'm seventy. Increasingly the future is pressing in, pressing in, reaching for me with long and cold fingers. I don't want to think about it. I don't want it to happen. I don't want to get old or fucking die, all right? And fuck you, Keith. Fuck you with your fucking questions and your sneer and your fucking recorder. I hate you and I hate all of the other small-minded patronising fuckwits like Phillip and half of the customers we get, all of those middle-aged fucking men with their rock-fucking-solid understanding of life and the world and how it all works and their wandering fucking eyes and wet mouths. Fuck them. Fuck them and fuck Keith and fuck Phillip. Fuck all of the Little Englanders that flock to pretty places – pretty places end up full of fucking sexists and bigots like Phillip. But it's not even just Phillip, is it? It's Keith as well, and he's not even from here, so it's not *here* that's the issue, it's just fucking people. Wherever they are, people ruin it. I'm sick of people, even here, where there aren't many people, I'm sick of them, and I'm sick of our towns and our cities and our countries and fucking national boundaries and all of the blood and war that they're built on. Not to mention the kind of perverse mentality behind what was done to Girt. The sadism. The whole fucking spectrum of aggression, it can all fuck off. It can go to Hell where it belongs. I don't want to be part of that species – the human race; I want out. I don't mean I want to die but I see what people do and I wish I was a fucking alien or something and I could just leave the planet and go home. I just don't get it. All the racism and xenophobia that exists despite human civilisation being such a brief blip in the face of the very land that we claim as ours to own, to control, with our flags and our border controls. Ownership is just spilled blood and that's the beginning and end of it. You can't have ownership without blood, just like you can't have magic without blood.

Fuck it. Fuck it all. The Candle can have me. It can have my blood. And I can put an end to Phillip's fucking creeping. That's something worthwhile that I can do. Something good I can do with my time, with my life. And so what if the Candle does well out of it? I hope it does. I hope it gets strong and fucks everything right up. I hope it overturns every convention, every dumb fucking human certainty.

I get a knife out of a kitchen drawer and immediately I feel calm. Yes, this was the right decision. I take the knife and sit on the sofa. I turn it over in my hands and look at it. I look down it from the end, and across it from the side.

I place the sharp edge – and it is sharp, very sharp – across my wrist, but I don't press down.

I need somewhere that will bleed, but not too much – I don't want to end up brain-damaged, or dead. Nor do I want to have to call an ambulance. That would be embarrassing, and everybody would get completely the wrong idea.

I put the knife back down and put Bob Marley on. 'No Woman No Cry'. I take a small plastic tub out of a cupboard and tap it against my lips as I pace up and down. I think about it. Head wounds always bleed badly; I remember once a tourist got very drunk and fell over on the road outside; he hit his head and his T-shirt ended up soaked with blood, but he was okay. He went to hospital and the cut turned out to be not that deep.

So maybe I could nick myself somewhere on the head – but it would be hard to control where the blood went; hard to direct it into any kind of receptacle. Maybe I could give myself a nosebleed? Though the thought of putting the knife up my nose gives me the heebie-jeebies. Nor do I want to hit myself in the face or anything. No, that's not going to work.

I pick up the knife and sit back down. I look again at my arm. I just need to choose a place that I can cut deeply without the risk of severing an artery.

Without thinking about it any longer, I grab the knife and slice it across the side of the crook of my arm. For a moment there's nothing to see and it doesn't hurt either, then the blood wells up and the pain arrives.

I bend my arm in an attempt to direct the flow of blood into the tub, then I shut my eyes tight and try to focus on my breathing. The pain feels hot and sharp and clean, like a kind of anger. But *breathe*. White spots move behind my eyes. *Breathe, Edie: focus on your breathing*. One, two, three, four, one, two, three, four, one, two, three, four, and on, and on, and on, and on.

The real pain does not last long and when I look I see that the cut is actually quite shallow. It has bled, some, and I have a little blood in the tub, but I squeeze the wound a bit in order to get some more. It still hurts, but it's far from unbearable.

It was kind of a stupid place to cut myself because it means that whenever I use my left arm it'll hurt, and the cut won't heal. But I suppose it also means that I might be able to use the same cut repeatedly. I wind some gauze around it – I have a first-aid kit here in the caravan – and roll my sleeve back down. I look at the blood in the tub. It's a few millimetres deep. I hope it's enough. I dip my little finger in and lick it. It tastes of money. I open the door and put the tub underneath the caravan, out of the rain. I guess somehow the Candle will know that I've done it.

I get back inside and close the door.

I am woken by a sound. At first I think it is just the rain, but no, there is something else: something moving outside. I can feel the Candle's closeness. I can hear it dragging itself along the ground, moving underneath the caravan. I sit up in bed. The rain beats down on the roof. From the floor, I can hear animal sounds, snuffling and snorting and gobbling, and scraping, as if it's pressed against the bottom of the caravan. I get out of bed and go to the door, ready to open it and see, but as my hand touches the handle, the Candle suddenly scampers off and in my head I hear laughter and a confusion of voices, and somewhere in there is a whispered *thank you, thank you, thank you,* and then the voices fade away, and now the Candle has gone, and I'm left with the rain.

CHAPTER NINE

There is a ruin in Ravenglass. It used to be a Roman bath-house. I like to go there sometimes and touch the stones and think about all of the people who've touched them since it was built. I imagine all of the walls and the roof standing and intact, and the rooms full of hot water and steam and Roman soldiers far from home.

At night the taller sections stick up against the sky: giant black shapes where the stars should be. In those taller sections there are archways that I like to walk through, trailing my hands along the crumbly fur of lichen that coats everything.

It is night and I am at the ruins, looking up at the sky and the stars. I remember the stars; I remember being amongst them, between them – I can't articulate the memory. Memory might not even be the right word; it's more *recognition*: recognition of these stars but from a different place, or from another angle. Everything is frosted and glittering. The first frost of the year.

I stand up – I didn't realise that I'd been lying down. I open my arms out wide and strain them upwards. Although I know these ruins, I feel as if I am looking at them through different eyes. There is a part of me that has just found this place, a part to which these ruins are new.

I head through the new ruins, coming out onto the small road that leads through the woods to the caravan site. Small things drop from the canopy overhead. Flies gradually accumulate and their drone increases in volume. Beyond the trees there are fields and beyond those are more trees – dead and bleached. Occasionally I smell smoke.

It's a still night. I creep onto the caravan site, which is where the tourists hang around and sleep between walking on the fells, standing on the beach and riding on the La'al Ratty. There's nobody around.

Some of the caravans have lights on and a couple have their doors open. There are a few static mobile homes along one edge of the site, raised up on breezeblocks, with canopies and hanging baskets and deckchairs outside. I slip between them, keeping low whenever I pass a lit window. Sometimes I hear the sound of quiet voices on radio or TV. I don't know what I'm doing here. I don't know what I'm looking for.

There: a man sitting in a garden chair outside his caravan, his head lolling to one side. I circle around him at a distance, and yes, he is asleep. He is wearing jeans and a baggy jumper.

A grimy shirt collar is visible at his neck. He is thin and balding, but has a ponytail of greying hair. He smells of drink, and his chair is surrounded by empty, crumpled beer cans. It looks as if he's been stamping on them, squashing them into discs. His caravan door is not quite closed.

I look around. I can hear laughter and low voices drifting through the clear, blue night air: people leaving friends to return to their own caravans, perhaps, or a couple stepping outside for a smoke. Whatever they're doing, they're not in sight yet, and they can't see me here.

I move in quickly, grab the drunk man under his armpits and haul him towards the door of his flimsy home. The door crashes open and I throw him into the darkened interior, which – like him – stinks of old, stale tobacco. I shut the door behind me. I'm not used to being so strong.

The man has woken up and now he's moaning. 'Hey,' he's saying, 'no need – no need. Who are you anyway?'

I don't say anything in return, but I watch as he flails his arms around, rubbing at his face and struggling to his knees. It's pretty dark in here so he won't be able to see who I am. He wouldn't know me anyway.

Empty beer cans litter the floor in here just as they litter the ground outside. Ashtrays are overflowing. A stack of tabloids are slowly yellowing in the corner. On the wall is a small framed picture of the man with a little girl.

He is standing now, a hand held to his head. I smack it away and grab his wrists and drive my thumbs through his palms, between the thin bones, stretching the tired old skin on the backs of his hands until it tears open and my thumbnails pop through. I push my thumbs right out and wiggle them around. It looks obscene. It's brilliant. It's the best thing I have seen in a long time. Blood runs from our union onto the floor. The man is screaming, but he can't get away now because we are attached. I rush him against the wall and headbutt him, so hard that the back of his head puts a dent in the caravan side. He stops screaming and falls limp. The bones in his hand feel like those of a chicken. I snap them by moving my thumbs briskly sideways. Then I shake him off me and let him fall to the floor. I reach down and open his mouth. I get a good firm grip on his tongue and start to rip it loose. He's still alive and he twitches, though I don't think he's conscious now, which is good because I don't want him screaming any more. The man's teeth are already loose – his gums have receded to almost nothing – and I knock a few of them out for good measure. I roll him over so he doesn't choke on the teeth or drown in the dark blood now pouring from the bottom of his mouth. I stamp on the base of his spine. I rip open first his clothes and then his skin and I get my hands inside him and rub them up and down his vertebrae.

Finally I pummel and squeeze at the muck and jelly of his internal organs.

Afterwards I wear his guts looped around my neck and paint the inside of the caravan with his blood and other fluids: long streaks and smears, handprints, flicks and speckling.

Nobody has come to investigate the earlier screaming – but that's normal, isn't it? You hear a scream, you tense up, you wait to see if it carries on, and if it does, then you know somebody's really in trouble and not just messing around. If it doesn't come back, well, it was probably somebody trying to scare somebody else, or maybe someone being tickled, or something.

I hop down from the caravan. Oh, what a clear night it is! A night like this gives you a real sense of time and space; it makes you glad to be alive. Being alive is the best thing there is. Those of us strong enough to live are lucky – but then, we deserve it. We *deserve* it.

My feet are light upon the frost as I leave the caravan site. Where am I going? I could go anywhere.

Chapter Ten

I've never had a vision quite as immediate as that before. I'm always *watching;* I never take part. Things are changing – or maybe I did it. I could have gone sleepwalking and done it in my sleep. I've lived on my own for so long now that for all I know, I am a sleepwalker; I could have been doing it all these years and nobody would have told me. I once read about a man who drove to his mother's house and killed her, all in his sleep. I don't know if people believed him, but apparently his grief appeared genuine, and no motive could be established.

But no; my feet are clean and there is no blood under my fingernails. I look around the caravan – *my* caravan, that is, not the one in which the man was killed – for bloody clothes, but find nothing.

I don't know why I'm questioning what's happened. If I

stop thinking for a moment, the answer becomes obvious: it was the Candle. It had to be the Candle.

I know it was the Candle in the same way that I know the Candle exists at all: because it is there in my mind, when I let myself see it. I visualise my mind as an ocean: when I'm thinking hard, the waves are high, tumultuous, and visibility is much reduced. When I calm down and stop thinking so much, the waves disappear and the water becomes very flat and still – a lot flatter and stiller than any ocean in reality – and I can see further, and that's when I see the light of the Candle, hovering, and that's when I learn things from that light – although perhaps 'learn' is the wrong word, because that suggests effort. Once I am aware of the Candle, it is no effort at all to realise certain truths. It's just a case of being open-minded.

It's a cold October morning, and I've got to do breakfasts.

I get the bacon out of the packet and linger, holding it in my hand, pinching it between thumb and forefinger. I don't know if I have ever really appreciated the grain of the meat before, the smell of it, the satisfying give of it.

And the eggs: the sound of the shells breaking; the way the whites spill out stringily, like something from that open gullet. I stand and break one after the other, shivering slightly with every small crunch, fascinated by the viscosity of the fluid, until the fryer is covered with the white and yellow mess of too many eggs, the first ones now blackening around the edges, burning, and there is no room for the tomatoes or other foods.

Maria comes into the kitchen before the breakfasts are finished. 'I was just walking through,' she says, 'and Mr Bull asked for another pot of tea.' She looks at me and puts a hand on my shoulder. 'What's wrong? You look very bad.'

For a moment I look at her, wondering how she can tell, thinking that she means bad morally, ethically, as if she is saying I look evil – but no, she doesn't mean that.

'Ha,' I say, 'yeah, thank you. No, I feel bad. I was ill through the night. I didn't sleep.'

'Your hands are shaking.'

I look down. She's right. 'Yeah,' I say.

'I want to give you some time off,' she says.

'No,' I say, 'I want to work.'

'Are you sure?'

'I need to keep busy,' I say. 'I need the structure at the moment, and I need to keep my brain going. I'm not very well, you're right, but I don't think I want the opportunity to dwell on it any more than I do already. I should just work through it.' I offer a weak smile. 'The Devil makes work for idle hands, and all that.'

Maria gives me a hug. 'Well,' she says, 'just let me know what I can do.'

After work, back in the caravan – in *my* caravan – I open up the laptop and try to occupy myself, but after about half an hour I turn the thing off and put some music on instead and try reading.

I don't know why it takes me so long, but slowly I realise that there is a way of finding out what really happened last night. I'm lying there, headphones on, but no music playing, e-reader in hand, but not reading anything, looking up at the ceiling, and I realise it's simple: I can go to the caravan site, see for myself. Go and put my mind at rest.

Obvious.

I get up, put on my shoes and my coat. Outside, in the shadow of the pub, the grass is still white with frost. My breath mists.

There are no police at the caravan site, though it could just be that nobody's spotted anything yet.

I didn't take the route that was taken last night. There are people like Mitchell and his mother, who live in the static caravans, who might recognise me should they look out of the window as I pass. Instead, I go for a more circuitous route, walking around the opposite edge of the field, around the holidaymakers. There are people around, but not many; midweek in October, places like this are empty. A few people are packing rucksacks, cleaning their expensive walking boots, heating up beans over camping stoves. I don't draw their attention, and none of them appear to notice me; though it's possible people here might recognise me from the pub, it's not very likely.

They're all carrying on as they normally would. Maybe nobody knows what happened. Maybe nothing did happen.

I recognise the caravan from a distance. It's next to the currently empty part of the site, so there is nobody near the side of the caravan where the man was sitting.

The caravan door is not quite shut. I can see blood on the step, and blood on the grass around the deckchair, dried to glossy brown. Through the small window I can see that the lace curtain that was white is now splashed with red. I sink to my knees, but then get right back up again and turn around. I can't stay here: somebody might see me. I have to go. I have to *go*.

I force myself to walk, not run, back to The Tup.

So the Candle did this. The Candle killed a man. And I helped it. I'm inside my caravan leaning against the door and smoking. This is what the Candle wanted to be stronger for, then. Killing. Not just killing, but *savaging*. It was a monstrous act; obviously I know it was monstrous, but I am not as repulsed or as disgusted or as dismayed as I should be, because I shared what the Candle felt at the time: enthusiasm, pleasure, *joy*. Those emotions have seeped into me. When I think about the skin splitting and the bones breaking and the blood spraying, the Candle's exultation flares briefly deep within.

And then there is the gift it is giving me; the means to prove Phillip's crimes. If Phillip did kill that girl all those years ago, then he is a murderer, and he could still have murder in him. With the Candle's help I will prevent that. In balance, in the long term, the Candle's presence here could result in less death, not more.

But still, rationalisation aside, the Candle's happiness burns in me.

I'm down to the cigarette's filter. I stub it out on the worktop; I realise that I've just been letting the ash fall down on to the floor.

Later that night I think about Phillip. I see him sitting at his computer, blogging, typing actually quite fast. Small droplets of sweat fall onto his keyboard.

I see him brushing his big yellow teeth, just standing there, thinking about something else while his hand moves rhythmically. I can't see his thoughts. I guess at them. Perhaps thinking about a female cyclist he photographed in the rain in the blue early morning, or perhaps about a girl that worked in the office that he used to work in.

Toothpaste foams down his chin, all over his hand and down his forearm before dropping into the sink in big, wet, saliva-laden globs. The bathroom mirror is almost totally obscured by dried flecks of toothpaste and there are brown tidemarks in the sink. He keeps on brushing and brushing, as if he's in a trance. Minutes pass, and then more minutes.

CHAPTER ELEVEN

When Mitchell arrives the following evening, he's out of breath.

'You okay?' I ask. Tonight'll be busy, so I'm preparing some more vegetables in advance, chopping carrots, cabbages, cauliflower – nothing very exciting.

'I ran here,' he says, panting. He's got terrible skin at the best of times, but tonight his acne is livid. 'Loads of bloody journalists or reporters or whatever at the site, trying to ask questions. It's horrible, Edie, they keep knocking on the caravan. Mum won't go outside and Dad's getting dead angry. And they followed me here.'

'So they're with the million and one who're already in the bar, then?'

'Aye.'

'It'll be busy tonight, Mitchell.'

'Aye, but people aren't coming out, Edie. Apart from the

journalists and reporters. Everyone who lives here – they are all staying in, aren't they?'

'I suppose so,' I say. But why didn't they stop coming out on Wednesday? Of course, I knew about the murder before anybody else. It wasn't reported until after I'd checked the caravan out. The news of Mr Aiden Bell's death broke yesterday, and it was only last night that people started to hear the word 'murder', and it was only this morning that a few of the gory details started getting passed around. And apart from the media people that all arrived en masse today, the bar is actually very quiet. Mitchell's right.

I can imagine the headlines already: PICTURESQUE SEASIDE TOWN RIVEN BY MYSTERIOUS MURDER. MAN FOUND EVISCERATED IN MOBILE HOME. CARAVAN CARVE-UP. RIPPED UP IN RAVENGLASS. FINGERS AND THUMBS. TONGUE-TIED HOMICIDE.

When Maria comes in with the first order I get a glimpse of the bar beyond. Lots of people are huddled around the tables, grinning. Lots of teeth.

Things get really bad with Saturday's papers. There's a picture of the inside of the caravan in a few of the tabloids. I don't get it; I don't want to believe that the police would have leaked the image, or let someone in with a camera. It's just as graphic and awful as you'd expect. And the accompanying words are no better.

I'm in the kitchen after serving breakfast to the jackals

and I can hear more and more of them turning up, asking Maria for rooms. By midday she's turning them away. It must be the pictures: I get the sense that this isn't your ordinary murder. Unless it's always like this in places where somebody's been killed. After Derrick Bird killed twelve people on his shooting spree, West Cumbria was thick with reporters. They were all over the place like a rash. People who knew Bird, or knew the victims, were being chased from their cars to their doorsteps by journalists wanting exclusive information.

I pick up a few of the papers from the bar, not making eye-contact with anyone in an attempt to avoid conversation, and then leave the building via the kitchen and head for my caravan. There's a note tacked to the door.

EDIE - ANY INFO RE MR BELL?
WOULD LOVE TO CHAT. 07786 356399. KEITH X

I throw the note straight in the bin when I get inside, and open one of the tabloids and see a story – a column – about Mr Bell that also mentions Girt's death:

> The viciously dismembered body of a local alco-
> holic has been discovered just a few miles from
> the site of a satanic animal slaughter, on the
> doorstep of controversial nuclear reprocessing
> plant Sellafield. Aiden Bell, 57, described by locals

as 'a bit of a loner', was fired from Sellafield for
negligence. Police are not publicly linking Mr
Bell's death with the ritualistic slaying of Girt, the
dog found . . .

There is no news in the article, not for me. I know the
details of the death, and as for the paper's speculation
regarding Mr Bell – it's a waste of space. I jump to the
Comment piece.

. . . the terrible, arcane things happening in such
a picturesque little village? What sordid goings-
on connect the two deaths? This paper has, in the
past, drawn your attention to some of the more
unsavoury elements of youth culture and the
prevalence of occultism and supernatural violence
in modern computer games. Is it too hard to
imagine impressionable teenagers being inspired
to read up on some of these practices after encoun-
tering them in a virtual world? Is . . .

I can't read any more. There's something especially unset-
tling about this when they're discussing something close
to home. I close the paper.

Over the next few days – as the police repeatedly announce
that they're 'following up leads' but produce no prime

suspects – the media presence grows even larger, and solidifies, somehow. There are more reporters than there are tourists, filling up the guesthouses and bed and breakfasts, and they stay into the new week. On Monday night there are as many journalists in the pub as contractors; they line up along the bar and ask Maria questions she can't and won't answer.

The bar pretty much becomes their territory. They're all shouting over each other and laughing into mobile phones – until they spot a local, that is, and then they swarm. I stop going in there after my shift and instead retire to my caravan, where I go online to find out what nonsense they've all been making up.

On the nights that Gabe works, he gets a disproportionate amount of attention from the media people. The questions are getting more aggressive, and one skinny drunken specimen shouts, 'Killed any dogs recently?' on an almost hourly basis.

By the end of the week Gabe's taken to wearing a shirt and tie instead of his customary *Converge* and *Dillinger Escape Plan* hoodies, but it's too late. I can hear them through the kitchen door: 'Wearing a disguise, are we?' the skinny man sneers. I don't hear Gabe respond – I imagine he's following Maria's lead and keeping his mouth shut – but I can hear Phillip's laughter, that abrasive *hee-haw*, loud above the hubbub.

These guys all eat a lot of meat. I clatter plate after loaded plate onto the side and Mitchell and Gabe do the waiting.

A couple of hours into the shift I realise I haven't spoken a word all night. Neither Mitchell nor Gabe are very conversational either; Gabe's face is a thin-lipped mask. I want to say something to him, but I don't know what.

'Edie,' Maria says later, as I'm putting together the last order of the shift, 'come through for a drink after that. I need some decent company out here. I can't bear it alone.'

'Maybe we should close up,' I say. 'We should kick them all out and close up – maybe the whole village should close up. It's not respectful for us all to carry on like this, and it's probably not safe either.'

Maria looks at me, hands on hip, head cocked. 'Edie,' she says, 'you know I can't close up. These people are scum' – she lowers her voice to a whisper – 'but we all need to eat.'

'You whispered the wrong bit, Maria.'

'You can still smile then?' she says. 'Good. I was worried.'

'Aren't you scared, though?' I ask. The last plate of food lies cooling between us, but I couldn't give a fuck. Those people out there should be eating out of troughs anyway; they don't deserve to have anything nice cooked for them. I suppose the fact they're paying for it makes some kind of difference. I suppose that's what money means.

'Scared?' Maria says. 'I don't know. Yes, a bit. But I don't really believe that there is some kind of serial killer out and about. I mean, there's nothing to suggest that, is there?

Nothing to suggest that there wasn't a personal motive. On the crime shows they always look for a reason for murder.'

'I suppose so,' I say after a beat. But that random man was killed for pure joy, or something like joy, and curiosity. After a couple of days I realise I can articulate the feeling a little bit more clearly: it felt like a type of hunger, a kind of *I've missed this. I wonder if I can still* . . .

'I suppose so,' I repeat.

I do as Maria asks and slip through into the bar once I'm done. I pull myself a pint of Dizzy Blonde, sit down on the one empty bar stool – the one next to Phillip, naturally – and avoid making eye-contact with any of the assorted journalists. I think they must know that the murder was not simply some personal vendetta or anything like that; the way they've all descended on the place, they're expecting more to come. And if they suspect Satanism or some such nonsense, then they've got the opportunity for a good old moral panic on their hands. They could spin it out for weeks, even if nothing else happens.

But something else will happen. I know it.

Dizzy Blonde is a terrible name for a beer, but the beer itself is good. There is a casual misogyny evident in the naming of ale; so many have names like Dizzy Blonde or Wood Nymph or Dusky Maiden. There are no Strapping Brickies or Suave Gents, or – I don't know. My ideas are no less stupid than the breweries'. It's not as if I want any kind of man. I suppose not all men are looking for women. I don't know.

If I was going to give a beer an anthropomorphic name, a male name, I'd probably call it Spike, after Spike in *Buffy the Vampire Slayer*. Or – no. That's just stupid.

'Edie,' Gabe says, waving a hand in front of my face. 'Edie!'

'What?'

'At last! I've been saying your name for ages. I thought you were drunk or dead or asleep with your eyes open.'

'I was thinking,' I say.

'What about?'

'*Buffy the Vampire Slayer* – remember that?'

'Remember it?' he says quietly. 'I learned to wank watching Buffy.'

I shake my head. 'Jog on,' I say. 'Pure filth. Go on, get away. Are you supposed to be collecting glasses or what?'

'You love it,' he says. 'Anyway, you're the only one around here I can talk to about that kind of stuff.'

'You don't have to talk about wanking at all, Gabe.'

'Sometimes you do.'

'What about your friends? You know, Billy, David and – the other one. Ed.'

Gabe shakes his head. 'I don't know,' he says. 'They don't get me like you do.'

My mouth drops open and he smiles – his first smile of the week – and heads off to collect glasses. I watch him go.

I didn't realise I got him at all. I didn't realise we were close.

The media types become less persistent the more they drink; they're all slumped around by eleven o'clock, just talking to each other. Maintaining that degree of aggression and insensitivity must be quite exhausting.

I say that, but Phillip's still going strong, loudly regaling Keith with a story about how, once, Gabe and his friends were playing Dungeons and Dragons in the bar. They're laughing as if this is inherently hilarious.

It was the first and last time Dungeons and Dragons came into The Tup. It's a shame. It was a good idea.

Gabe is hovering near them, busying himself with something behind the bar, pretending not to listen. Maria is genuinely not listening.

'Hey,' I say, 'give it a rest, Phillip. You whine when you see the boys sitting out on the benches, but if it wasn't for you they'd feel at home in here.'

'Oh, Edie,' Phillip says, 'you're so tolerant, aren't you? So understanding. Well, I happen to be honest enough to acknowledge that there's some behaviour I find ridiculous. If Gabe's going to be so infantile and weird then I don't see why we shouldn't have a laugh about it.' He raises his voice. 'Maybe it'll teach him to stop messing around with all these games and start doing something worthwhile with his life!'

Gabe looks up at Phillip. 'I take it you're not trying to find a decent job at the moment, then?' he asks.

'A decent job?' Phillip sneers. 'Beggars can't be choosers, my lad. When you're old enough you get any old job and eventually, if you're lucky, you might work your way up or find a better one. That's how it works.'

'Maybe that's how it works if you've got no ambition and want to grow up into a miserable old fuckwit,' Gabe says, looking back down at the glass-washer. 'I know that's what you might consider worthwhile, but not me.'

Phillip's face is usually wide-open, even when he's trying to be subtle, but right now it's hard to read.

Keith clears his throat. 'Look, Gabriel,' he says, 'I don't think you're in a position to be lecturing anybody at the moment. Not after what you've done.'

'What?' Gabe smiles. 'What have I done?'

'We all know what you've done,' Keith says. 'I'm talking about the dog.'

'I didn't do anything to Girt!' Gabe shouts.

Maria is watching now.

'Come on, son,' Keith says, 'you and your friends – it doesn't take a genius to see that you're the most likely culprits, does it? We all know that when you're young it's easy to be seduced by certain – ideas, shall we say? Everyone knows you and your friends play around with – well, let's say the darker end of the spectrum—'

'What are you talking about?' Gabe says. 'Are you talking

about Dungeons and Dragons? Do you know how stupid you're being?'

'You're a violent little pervert,' Phillip snarls suddenly, spitting as he does so. 'What kind of creep enjoys those video games you play? I've looked at them on the internet – if you can get pleasure from that, then who knows what you're capable of? You and your mates, you'll be in that Black Circle Society people talk about.'

'Wait,' I say, 'Phillip: you go on the internet and look up things that Gabe likes? Why do you do that? And what's the Black Circle Society?'

'You fuck off, bitch,' he says, turning to me. 'The dyke sticking up for the deviant? How touching – how predictable. How *pointless*. Get this into your thick head, sweetheart: we don't give two shiny shites what you think about anything.'

I don't know what to say. I look at Keith and catch a brief smirk flitting across his face.

The whole pub is silent now. The assembled news crews are fascinated, no doubt.

'Barred,' Maria says, breaking the silence. 'You are both barred. Now get out, both of you – right now. And Phillip: you are not welcome back, never. I never want to see you in here again.'

'Don't worry,' Phillip says, 'I don't want to be served food by you jam rolls anyway. Especially him.' He points at Gabe and slides from his bar stool. 'You killed that dog and I know you killed that man as well, and soon everyone will know. You're a dirty little scumbag with no morals, no sense of right and wrong.'

'Probably left 'em on the boat,' Keith snorts.

Gabe is always pale anyway, but now he's virtually translucent. There's a sheen of sweat on his forehead and I can see dark patches under his arms. I want to ask again what the Black Circle Society is, but it's not the right time.

'Everyone's going to know you for the stinking pervert you are,' Phillip says, struggling with his coat. 'The stinking, murderous—'

'Hey,' I say. I put my hand on Phillip's shoulder. 'You're breaking the law by saying that. That's sla—'

He backhands me across the face and I fall backwards off the tall bar stool. It doesn't hurt so much at first. Instinctively I bent my neck so as not to hit my head on the stone floor, but lying there I taste blood, and then it's running over my lips and I realise that my nose and something in my mouth are both bleeding.

As I stand up, I see Gabe breaking the top off a pint glass on the edge of the bar.

'No,' I say, but my voice is quiet. I clamber to my feet.

Gabe sticks the remains of the glass in Phillip's face and Phillip howls, his arms windmilling. I see the beautiful, sharp curves slice into his mottled cheek and, as his skin parts, a small part of me exults. The red of his blood is so bright and vivid that it's almost psychedelic, hallucinatory.

He screams and Keith screams and Maria screams. Blood pours down Phillip's face from a wound on his forehead. I wonder if any of the glass went into his eye.

'Polack cunt!' Keith screams at Gabe. 'Fucking Pole!'

Gabe just looks stunned as blood runs down from the glass onto his white hand. Cameras are going off all over the place and everyone's talking at once.

Keith throws a punch at Gabe and hits him square on the jaw, and Gabe just falls. I grab Keith's thick curly hair and kick him in the back of the knee and he collapses, so that I'm carrying the weight of him by his hair. Then Maria is there, and she's grabbing Keith's balls and squeezing them and shouting into his face, 'Get out! Get out!' so frenziedly that there's no gap between the words.

I can't hear anything else, but I'm aware of Phillip on his knees, his mouth open, still bleeding copiously from the wide-open cuts on his face.

After the police have been and taken statements, and after Maria and I have cleaned up, I go to bed, and the sound of Phillip's hand on my face comes back to me: the sound of a tenderiser hitting a fresh steak, hard, solid, flat, wet. I hear it again and again, so clearly it's as if there's somebody out there in the dark, outside the caravan, standing with a heavy lump of meat in one hand and a hammer in the other, bringing them together again and again, just for me. I don't know the last time I got a proper night's sleep.

The world outside the caravan is dark. I sit on the edge of my low bed and look at the tiny window and start to blink and rock and sweat as I try to picture the world beyond – the world that it might have become since I closed the door. I pick at the cut on my arm; it hasn't had a chance to scab over, as I re-open it every other night.

Chapter Twelve

There are no tourists dressed in bright waterproofs riding bikes towards the railway bridge today, no bored children being dragged to antique fairs, no busy guesthouses. The sulphuric smell of the La'al Ratty is heavy in the air, despite the breeze. What sky that can be seen through the ragged sheet of grey cloud is cold blue.

I'm walking from The Tup towards the chandlery and the beach. The houses I pass all have their curtains drawn. The blue benches on the grassy embankment are empty. There are no families looking out over the estuary; there is no ice-cream van. There's nobody sitting at picnic tables with pints from the pub looking up at the huge sky.

I head up some concrete steps to stand on the embankment. The blue metal handrail is decorated with a Viking ship design and there are vessels out on the water: catamarans and fishing boats and small yachts. Orange buoys float listlessly. I can smell the sea. Over the estuary, in the distance beyond the rise of the far shore, I can see a tower at Sellafield rising from the haze. To the right is the railway bridge; beneath the bridge is only darkness. Water flows into and out of this darkness, depending on the tide. You can stand on the bridge – there's a narrow footbridge that hangs off it – and watch the water flowing around the vast support columns, watch the weeds pulled this way and that. I touch my swollen lip, my black eye. Phillip hit me hard.

I walk further down the road, past the Post Office with its window so covered in small notices that you can't see in or out. I peer in through the door, but it doesn't look like there's anybody there.

I haven't seen anyone since I left the pub, no movement through windows, nothing.

Seabirds call out above me.

The houses that line this road are low, narrow things, adorned with ceramic ornaments and extravagant name and number signs. Wind-chimes tinkle and hanging baskets creak in the breeze. Long fronds of various creeping plants trail down walls.

There are houses on either side of the road, then the road turns into a ramp down onto the sand. The chandlery, on the left of the ramp, is almost buried beneath a mountain of lobster pots draped in seaweed. The big blue double doors are open. I look inside, but Edward – the chandler – doesn't seem to be around. There's a big dinghy occupying most of the space, and a filthy quad bike taking up the rest. If you didn't know it was a shop you wouldn't be able to tell. Various boating tools hang from the walls.

Shining out of that back-of-the-room gloom is a row of long, sharp knives. I'm looking at them before I know what they are.

I blink and back away.

To the right of the ramp is a high, grey, pebble-dashed wall, which curves around the back of the houses and protects them from the beach. On it is a big white sign, with red writing on it.

WARNING NOTICES

YOUR ATTENTION IS DRAWN
TO THE MOD ESKMEALS BYELAWS

1) Guns are fired over the foreshore out to the sea from the land area shown on the byelaws. Entry by unauthorised persons to this land area is prohibited at all times.

2) Access to the shore and sea shown on the byelaws is prohibited when the red flags are flying, subject to the exemptions contained in the byelaws. At other times access is permitted.

3) It is dangerous to touch or disturb any shell, bomb, missile or strange object found on the sands or beach. Please report its approximate position at the first opportunity to the establishment.

I'm never sure which 'establishment' is being referred to on the sign. The MOD? The police? The notices are accompanied by a small map showing which area is out of bounds completely, and which is out of bounds when the red flags are flying.

Here, on the beach itself, the squealing of seabirds is getting louder. I look around for people – fishermen sorting their boats out or digging for lugworm; dog-walkers; kids with kites – but there's no one.

There's not really any sand here; it's more a kind of sandy mud, strewn with pebbles and empty shells. A terrible eggy smell hangs in the air, the steam railway smell, but coupled with something else more organic. There are a few empty cars parked at odd places on the sand, almost as if people were driving around the beach and then were suddenly raptured away, leaving their vehicles behind. There are boats here too, beached and tilting in the silt. Grey wooden posts stick up near the high wall and people who live in those little houses have stretched washing-lines out from their back yards to these mollusc-encrusted bone-like things. A huge rusted anchor rests on the surface of the mud. I always assumed the anchor was supposed to be some kind of monument or sculpture – I thought it was a bit big to have simply been discarded near the ramp – but it's been left to shift and deteriorate with the tides over the years, and so I've changed my mind.

When I look forwards, I see that the mud and the sea

and the horizon and the sky and the clouds are all flat and horizontal, layered up one on top of the other, like strata in rock.

I sit down on the anchor and listen out for the sound of another human being.

Ravenglass is a place people come on holiday. I understand it, I think; it's the kind of place where you feel alone, out of touch – that's what I like about it. And it's an ideal location if you want to get up into the mountains and valleys; what with the little railway and the remnants of Roman occupation, it's great for historians and people who get excited about that kind of thing. But when you sit and look at it, when you look around, it's desolate. You can romanticise these places, but if you're in the wrong frame of mind they're lethal.

The breeze picks up and I button my coat and pull my beanie hat further down. The salt in the air is getting into my split lip and it's hurting. At least I think it's the salt; maybe it's some kind of chemical weapon the MOD are testing at Eskmeals – maybe that's what the smell is. I look at the stones on the beach and wonder if any of them are ammo casings, washed up here at Ravenglass – rather than in the prohibited zone – as the result of some erroneous calculation by the scientists.

If I don't turn around I'm at the end of the world. I'm the last living person. Fuck it, even if I do turn around, there's nobody there. All these cars and boats and anchors and washing-lines and strange little houses are no more indicative of human presence than that tumbledown Roman bathhouse or the stone circle at Greycroft. I am alone; I will be alone for ever.

How would this particular end of the world happen? Nuclear war, probably, started over resources – oil, food, I don't know. I'd watch the sky light up at night, hear the roaring of bombs and think *I'm glad I never fell in love and had kids.* I'd think *it's only a matter of time until the war gets me.* There would be mushroom clouds on the news and eventually I'd see one in real life. I'd be sitting right here on this anchor, looking out to sea, and there it would be: a bright light to the north. I'd turn my head and see a small lightbulb hovering in the air a few inches from my face. Then it would grow, and I'd realise it wasn't just a few inches from my face, but in the distance. The sky above it would light up; sharp shadows would be cast on the ground, all pointing at me. The air would bulge out around it. What clouds there were would bend upwards. It would be as if the whole world was a soft screen and something was trying to push through. Then the bulb would darken and stretch, and the top would break away and roll up above the fiery column, the whole thing growing and growing, and the sound would wash over everything, and as the birds fell out of the sky I'd sit here on this anchor, alone, and just wait for the light to hit me.

*　　　*　　　*

When I get back to the Tup, Maria is sitting at the bar with a white wine. The pub is closed. Gabe is with the police, and I think Phillip is too.

'You should have something stronger,' I say.

Maria just looks at me. I can tell she's looking at the damage. 'I'm so sorry, Edie,' she says, and puts her arms around me. 'I should have barred that awful man a long time ago.'

'You're forgiving,' I say. 'That's all.'

I feel her chest heaving and know that she's crying. There's no rush to do anything so I just stay there holding her for a while. 'Gabe will be okay,' I say eventually, but she doesn't say anything back and I think maybe I failed to sound convincing. 'How long are we staying closed?'

'I don't know.' She breaks the embrace and wipes her eyes. 'What do you think?'

'Day after tomorrow, we re-open for the evening. That's what I think.'

'You think people will come?'

'Yeah. I've just been for a walk and it's weird, Maria: there's nobody around – nobody at all. I think they're scared. But I think they'll want to be together if they can be.'

'You don't think they'll just want to stay at home, rather than walking around at night?'

I shrug. 'Mr Bell wasn't walking around at night,' I say. 'He was at home. No, I think people will want to be together. And it was like you were saying yesterday – there's no reason for anyone to believe that the murder wasn't just a one-off. A personal thing.' No reason for anyone else to believe that, anyway. 'Let's just see how it goes.'

'Some of the reporters have moved over to Rose Villa. Some are in the Pennington. I think some have gone home, but I reckon they'll be back, so I'm not going to have Gabe working here until it's all over. I don't want them to say those things to him any more. He didn't choose to come here.'

'You shouldn't have to tolerate it either,' I say. 'Choosing to come here has nothing to do with it.'

Maria thinks for a moment and then waves her hand. 'I know, I know. But he's only young. I feel responsible.'

I clamber over the bar and get another bottle of white wine out of the fridge.

Business does not disappear completely. The contractors are back, and there are quite a few locals in too – not Phillip though. I haven't seen hide nor hair of him since Saturday night. And Gabe's secluded himself away in his room since Sunday evening, when he returned from the police station. Phillip isn't pressing charges, probably because he knows that Gabe's attack was provoked by him hitting me, and that there are witnesses to this.

So Maria covers the bar and Mitchell and I cover the food.

'Dad's driving me to and from work now,' was the first thing Mitchell said when he arrived. 'It's about a thirty-second drive.'

'You know if there was a taxi firm round here, we'd pay for them to ferry you,' I said.

'I know.'

From the kitchen, everything sounds normal and happy in the bar. But when I go through, after I've finished, I find Maria almost vibrating with anger. 'People are talking,' she hisses.

I listen to the assorted conversations going on around the pub, catching only fragments: Mrs Cook is in, talking excitedly to Mrs Halliwell, and I hear her say something about a local 'peeping tom', and how she always thought 'Gabe was a lonely creature'. I hear breathless references to 'Polish culture' from one table and 'that poor Geordie lass' from another.

That gives me pause; I need Phillip to incriminate himself, and soon.

'People will talk,' I say. 'I know they shouldn't, but they will.'

'They should talk about things they bloody know about then,' Maria says. Her jaw is clenched.

'I'm not fighting with you,' I say. 'I agree. But you know what people are like.'

'Fucking stupid,' she says, 'that's what they're like.'

The next night also busy, and thick with rumours. It's better, though, because Pitbull joins us at the bar, rather than sitting with his contractor colleagues. He's wearing a black vest and greening tattoos spill out down his arms from beneath it – topless women and snakes and daggers and skulls – classic designs, haphazardly placed.

'People are reading about Satanic rites in the papers,' he says to Maria. 'They think your lad's involved too.'

'I know,' Maria says. She shakes her head. 'I know.'

'There've been stories about him assaulting an elderly local as well,' Jason says.

'Who?'

'Phillip,' I say.

'Oh, yeah,' Maria says, 'of course, but— Wait, you mean they've named him in the papers?'

'Yes. He's not a kid any more, and besides, Phillip isn't pressing charges. So it's not a legal matter.'

'Well,' Maria says, after a moment, pinching the bridge of her nose. 'My idiot son glassed a gobshite. There are gobshites all over. He should have known better.'

'He only did it because Phillip hit me, Maria,' I say. 'It wasn't unprovoked. He's not like that.'

Maria nods, but does not reply.

'So what's all this about a perv, then?' Jason asks. 'Everyone's talking about a perv.'

'It's been happening for a while,' I say. 'People – *women* – are saying they've seen someone watching them. Like, standing outside looking up at their windows. One girl said she saw this person sitting in a tree, looking straight into her bedroom.'

'I thought I saw him a few weeks ago,' Maria adds.

'We reckon some of the sightings are imagined, though,' I say, 'because no one's ever seen his face or been able to describe him. Everyone always says he runs off before they can get a good look, and it's always dark, of course. And it's easy to see things that aren't there in the dark, especially if you're thinking about them a lot already.'

'And do they reckon it's that rapist bastard?'

'Yeah,' Maria says. 'Well, he was never caught – forensics inconclusive, no witnesses, not a whole lot to go on. So people make that connection, between what happened to that girl and the peeper. But who knows. We don't know. Nobody knows.'

'The forensics were inconclusive because the girl's body was riddled through with eels,' I say.

Jason makes a face. 'Fucking hell, Edie,' he says, 'thanks! You're a real tonic.'

'It wasn't my Gabe,' Maria says. 'None of it.'

'We know that,' Jason says. 'Of course it wasn't Gabe.'

'He can't even go out any more!' Maria shouts, suddenly pointing at the door. 'Those reporters are chasing him down the street. Silly Sellafield weirdies are crossing the road to avoid him. People are calling him dog-killer, dog-fucker, pervert, rapist, murderer – and not even behind our backs!'

'Nothing gets people going like bad news, eh?' Jason says. 'Everyone's on about Mr Bell too. This weekend I've heard he's a spy who ripped himself apart after being given some kind of psychotropic drug, a gangster killed by some other gangster with attack dogs, a paedophile beaten to a smear by a group of vigilantes from Liverpool and – obviously, the tabloid favourite – killed as part of a devil-worshipping ritual or something.'

'It's all nonsense,' I say. 'It's just stupid. People should learn to keep their mouths shut.'

'They can't help it, though,' Jason says. 'It's interesting, innit? I mean, what happened to him – and why? I want to know as much as everyone. It's only natural—'

'It might be natural,' I say, 'but still . . .' I finish my pint. 'Right, then. I'm off to my little bed in my little house out back, so I'll say goodnight.'

'Edie, wait,' Maria calls. She's measuring out a round of whiskies for Nev and a couple of the other contractors. 'I want to run something by you.'

I wait by the kitchen door. I look up at the great big stag's head that's mounted on a shield-shaped piece of wood above the doorway to the men's loos. It is huge. Its antlers twist up and branch out into structures as complex and massive as trees. I feel like it's growing.

'Thanks, Edie,' Maria says when she comes over. 'Just a quick thing. I want to do something to kind of make up for what happened on Saturday. And just to cheer people up a bit, change what people are talking about. I was thinking a big bonfire might do it.'

'You don't have to make up for anything. You haven't done anything wrong.'

'No, but I feel like – it's a bad thing for a pub, to have had a glassing, but it's even worse when it's family. I mean, it could be the end for a place.'

'I think that's a good idea,' I say. 'For bonfire night, I take it?'

'Yeah. Bonfire, fireworks, free food – will you be able to handle that?'

'I'll need Mitchell and Gabe,' I say, 'and maybe somebody else to help serve.'

'Good. Thank you, Edie. You're a good girl.'

'No problem,' I say, and Maria smiles and returns to serve someone. I look quickly back up at the stag and nod good-night and head out through the kitchen.

I'm not really tired, so instead of going to bed I turn on the laptop and start browsing. Despite myself, I pay 'This Green and Pleasant Land' a visit. There's a new post, dated Sunday.

Feral Rats

Something is rotten, deep in the heart of rural England. Far, far away from the hustle and bustle of 'cosmopolitan' city centres, where you might expect to find mindless aggression and disturbing violence, in a little village called Ravenglass, the malignant forces of darkness have reached out and STRUCK! Yes that's right - dark forces, you heard me. You read that

correctly! I'm talking about the occult; about Satanism
or paganism or whatever the 'cool kids' are calling it
these black and Godless days.

You might have heard of Ravenglass already, what
with it being in the news. But what prompted me to
put pen to paper (or fingers to keyboard more like it,
haha!) was not the vicious murder that has drawn the
attention of citizens far and wide, no. It was another
incident - but one that I believe may be related........

You see, on Saturday night, a young man by the
name of Gabe Kowalski launched a mind-bogglingly
ferocious attack on a vulnerable, elderly regular at a
usually friendly rural pub. This young man (of Polish
extraction, it should be said) works at the pub in question. WHATEVER HAPPENED TO GOOD CUSTOMER
SERVICE!?!? I thought England was supposed to be
a 'service economy' these days for better or worse
instead it's more like a 'disservice economy', or even
a 'violent stabbing economy'!! One thing's for sure,
like death and taxes - I'm never going to tip again,
just in case I'm funding the narcotics habit of a
dangerous loony! But I digress!

My point is this: Gabe Kowalski is demonstrably
up to his neck in dangerous practices. Warped by
violent video games and the weird fantasy world of
Dungeons and Dragons, he and his friends dress in
hoodies with blood-spatter designs and listen to 'rock'

music that can only be described as DEMONIC SHRIEKING, it is so blood-curdling and horrible. According to the more upstanding residents of Ravenglass (for whom we must all have the greatest sympathy - we can all imagine all too well what it's like to watch your beautiful little village go entirely to the dogs) the youths loiter around the village at night smoking you-know-what and laughing at the moon like drunken pixies. They leave the stubs of melted candles in their wake - who knows what rituals they're performing? And more importantly, more pertinently - WHAT SACRIFICES ARE THEY MAKING?

Before you dismiss these questions as the rambling of a madman, let me tell you a bit more about Saturday night. I have it on good authority that the attack was entirely unprovoked and unjustifiable. The victim - a Mr Phillip Banks - was merely engaging Gabe in some ribald banter, as customers in a public house are wont to do with their bartender. Upon which, another member of staff - the dreadlocked and sanctimonious cook, Edie Grace - suddenly unleashed a savage tirade of bile all over Mr. Banks for no apparent reason. In retrospect, Mr Banks thought, it looked as if the two staff members had planned the attack in advance. When Mr Banks responded defensively, Edie Grace fell over as if punched; Gabe Kowalski then GLASSED

Mr Banks in the FACE!!! Ostensibly in retaliation to his striking Edie, which of course had not happened in the way Edie made it appear.

For those of you who are unaware, GLASSING is the act of smashing the rim off a glass and then using the remaining glass as a weapon. Yes, deeply unpleasant!! As you can imagine, Mr Banks has been left with deep scars and a partially paralysed face. THIS IS THE REALITY OF INTERGENERATIONAL RELATIONSHIPS IN TWENTY-FIRST CENTURY 'GREAT' BRITAIN, FOLKS! The youth have not only lost all respect, they have lost all goodness. Perhaps we cannot expect too much from those who, like Gabe, have been 'imported' from other cultures along with who-knows-what values and ideas. Perhaps these foreign ideas are poisoning our own young people? Who knows? Anything is possible in this modern world. One thing we can all be sure of though is that the youth of this nation are swiftly degenerating into a horde of FERAL RATS so desensitised that they have to get their kicks from BLOODY VIOLENCE and DEVIL WORSHIP. Have you SEEN the video games they play?

So, in light of what you now know - is it such a leap to suggest that Gabe Kowalski and his sinister cohort may have somehow been involved with the animal sacrifice at a local farm, or the sickeningly brutal murder of Mr Bell at Ravenglass caravan site? I think not. Willingness to shed blood indicates a cold-heartedness that must go hand-in-hand with the mindset requisite to be an occultist, and it also means that Gabe is capable of great violence.

I am sure you'll see much of this story in the papers over the coming days. Those of us who can still see the truth of things must once again shout it from the rooftops: SOFT-TOUCH LIBERALISM IS DESTROYING THIS COUNTRY!! What kind of MORONS can hear this kind of news and not take action to BAN VIOLENT VIDEOGAMES or refuse to CRACK DOWN ON OCCULTISM?? Can't they see that these FERAL RATS are OUT OF CONTROL?! There is BLOOD IN THE AIR, friends, and things are only going to get worse unless we STAND UP FOR WHAT IS RIGHT and tell the CRETINOUS PILLOCKS in Government that we, THE SILENT MAJORITY, demand to BE EMPOWERED!!!!

I close the laptop and shut my eyes. The mainstream coverage is more in line with this brainless online rant than I would have believed possible – though I suppose Satanism or what-ever makes for a good story. And no doubt the fact that Keith is spouting that nonsense through weightier publi-cations – the Red-tops – is influencing the slant of all the reporting.

And then I'm watching Phillip in his house. He's sitting at a dining table, working on a computer. The light from the screen is the only light in the room. His unwashed hair is greasy and his mauled face is twisted into an unthinking grin. I'm watching him through an open doorway, as if I'm lurking in the shadows of his kitchen. He's looking at his blog stats.

I focus on the screen as he closes his internet browser and opens up a folder. The folder is full of photos, and somehow, my perspective has changed so that I can see everything as if I'm looking over his shoulder. The photos are of Maria. Some of them have been taken in the bar, evidently with her knowledge, and she is smiling, covering her face, turning away. But some of them have been taken of her through the bedroom window. In most of these she is dressed, but in one she is only wearing underwear. There are a few photos of her naked, in the shower. There is video too.

Phillip attaches his camera to the computer and uploads some more. These new pictures are of Gabe. They have been taken at night, and they show him kicking back with his friends, smoking, hanging around the Roman ruins, playing video games, zoomed-in photos of the details of their hoodies.

Then there are photos of people I don't know, women, mostly, and mostly photos taken through windows, tourists, maybe, in various states of undress, many naked. There's even a couple making love. He has a very effective camera; the zoom must be really powerful for him to have got these pictures from the distance he must have been at. The details are pin-sharp.

There are photos of me, too, though thankfully none of me with no clothes on; the curtains in my caravan are heavy and bigger than the windows, and I know better than to get changed without making sure they're properly closed. But the photos show me at work in the kitchen and smoking outside The Tup. There are pictures of me with the Platts, too, standing in the yard on the day we buried Girt.

Phillip goes back to the folder where he stored the videos of Maria. He puts his hands to his crotch and unzips his fly, and then he pauses. All of a sudden he looks over his left shoulder, right into my eyes – or right where I feel like my eyes are – but he doesn't see anything. He turns back to his business.

I don't want to see any more, and, as soon as I think that, the vision recedes.

PART THREE

. . . a grand old house called Park Nook. Sometimes they threw great parties there, which would be the talk of the village for months afterwards. There were rumours that it was haunted — at one party, a guest was alone on one of the upper floors, looking for the lavatory, when she felt a hand reach out and grasp her own! I have never been inside that house myself, but I must confess to feeling curious — wouldn't it be something to see a ghost? Though, perhaps death hangs too heavily in the air already.

The house is very large and can be seen from the road, set behind an impressive lawn. The reason I remember it so well is that, in autumn, the edges of this lawn would be the best place — absolutely the best place — for finding conkers. The trees must be so old.

They're fantastic specimens Edith, very tall and statuesque, their branches spreading out over the road and the grass and, of course, at that time of year with all of the leaves turning to fire and drifting down through the woodsmoke air . . . there is a magic to that time of year, dont you think? As a young boy I'd be at my happiest kicking through the leaves, looking for those spiky green shells. Maybe if we live in Cumberland one day, and we are lucky enough to be blessed with a child, we could take them to Park Nook to look for the horse chestnuts? I imagine that house and those trees will stand forever . . .

CHAPTER THIRTEEN

I put two Sunday dinners down on a table in the bar and then, walking away, I am overcome with a vision of the stone circle, the stones black in the rain, the sea beyond them violent and rough, and the grass at the centre of the stones is darkening, as if it's being burnt, but I can't see any fire.

Every second night I freshen up the wound and squeeze a little more blood out into the tub. It is a little easier every time, and increasingly I use the knife to extend the length of the cut a little bit and thereby bleed a little more profusely. It gets to the point where the blood is usually about a centimetre deep, which looks okay to me, quite a healthy amount, not too much.

The nights roll by. I'm waiting for something, but I don't know what. The pub is busy in the evenings; the subject of the conversations stays much the same. Gabe remains sequestered. But people are relaxing. Basically, people are wondering what Mr Bell had done to instigate his own death. They are not thinking *maybe it will be me next*. They are thinking *he must have deserved it*. They don't use those words, of course, and it's possible they don't even articulate the sentiment so bluntly in their own heads, but at the moment it is the most common conclusion – nobody else has been killed, so he must have brought it down upon himself.

Maria prints some flyers for the bonfire and I go and stick one in the Post Office window. It's a Thursday and Ravenglass itself is still dead. The weather is getting colder and news of the murder and the glassing has put paid to most tourism for now, and until next summer, I imagine. I light up on the way back to The Tup and inhale deeply. Mid October. Where does the time go?

Before I get back to the pub my mobile starts ringing. It's John – John Senior.

'Edie,' he says, 'something bad's comin'.'

'What? Have you called an ambulance?'

'No, lass, nothing like that. Can you come up to the farm?'

When I get there, the kitchen door is open already. John Senior is pacing around, but when he sees me he strides over to the kettle and puts it on, despite the fact that it's obviously just boiled.

'What're you playing at?' he demands, turning and staring at me.

'What?' I say. Ice blooms inside.

'You know what,' he says, 'don't you.'

The kettle clicks off and John pours the hot water sloppily into two mugs on the crowded worktop. They look dirty, but I don't say anything.

'I don't think I do know what,' I say.

'They *told* me,' he says, jabbing his finger at me. 'They *told* me that something bad was coming and you're mixed up in it somehow. They were calling it the Elsewhere, and they were proper frightened. What's going on? I don't want you to get hurt, lass.'

'*Who* told you?'

'The fey,' he says, and with that second word, all of his energy abandons him and he collapses onto a kitchen chair. 'Those lasses at the tarn.'

I don't say anything. I hadn't really put much stock in his story of lights floating across Muncaster Tarn and turning into nymph lovers at first; I'd thought he was confused and drunk and remembering a dream, perhaps. But since then things have changed.

'They told me, Edie. What do you know?'

'I don't know anything! Why do you trust them, John?' I consider whether or not to pretend I don't believe him myself. 'How do you even know you're not imagining them?'

'I *know*,' he says. He fixes me with his eyes. 'And mark,

they said something bad is *coming*, not already here. We're not talking about poor old Mr Bell or Girt, we're talkin' about something else. The Elsewhere.'

This is what the Candle's doing, then.

'I have visions,' I say suddenly. 'I see things that are happening in other places, things that I shouldn't be able to see. I can't control it – or at least, I couldn't. I'm starting to be able to control it now, a little.'

'But you don't get given a gift like that without giving something back,' John says. 'I've read enough in all those books to know that much. What are you giving, and who are you giving it to, Edie?'

'You believe me, then?'

'Aye, of course I believe you. There's history around here, lass, a long history of strange things.'

'That tea'll be stewed,' I say.

'Hell's bells,' John says as he gets up. He sloshes milk into the mugs and grabs a teaspoon from the draining board and lifts the teabags out and drops them into the sink. 'We'll go through.'

'We used to hold séances back at Newton Manor,' John says, once we're ensconced in the other room, 'when we were young, like. Me and Christina and Mags and Don and others who've left the area since, or died. The couple who lived there, the Brettons, would have great big parties and we'd just turn up, even though we never really knew 'em. But that were the idea, that was the kind of party they held, and there'd always be a room with the lights turned off and a circle holding hands . . . It were only a matter of time before we started joining in. They called it the Black Circle Society. And then, when the parties stopped, we'd hold our own séances. We always kept close to Newton Manor, because it felt – they felt – more real there, like something might actually happen. That was where the magic was meant to be: Newton Manor, Greycroft, that area.'

He pauses for a moment to drink some tea, then asks, 'Are you cold, Edie?'

'Yes,' I say, though I hadn't realised it before he asked. I can hear the wind picking up outside.

'Could you get the fire going, lass? I'd do it, but I'm feeling my age.'

'No problem,' I say. I scrunch up the pages of a *Farmers Guardian* from last week and place them in the grate, then build a lattice of kindling on top of the balled-up newspaper and place a few lumps of coal on top of the edifice.

I always used to lay the fire at my grandparents' house. It was my favourite household job. It was the first thing I did every day, a real ritual: I'd riddle the grate, knocking all of yesterday's cold ash into the warped metal tray beneath so I could empty it into a bag and take it out to the big outside bin. Then I'd collect some kindling and build the fire, just like I've just done for John, and finally, I'd go and fill the coal scuttle so that there would be enough coal for the rest of the day. Grandma would have the kettle on, and she'd come through and say, 'Ooh, Edie, you're so good at laying the fire. I don't know what we'd do without you.' And she'd always add, 'You know Granddad'd do it himself, except for his hands.' If it was a cold day I'd light the fire then and there, making sure to put up the fireguard so that sparks didn't fly out and burn little black marks into the rug. It didn't matter that the rug was decades old and already covered in little black marks.

Until today I haven't built a fire since I moved out.

I light it with a match from a coal-blackened matchbox. I wipe my eyes dry before leaving the fire alone and returning to my seat.

John, oblivious, continues, 'Often nothing really did happen, even though we stuck to the grounds of Newton Manor. Y'know, the outhouses, the ice-house, those little buildings.' It takes me a moment to realise that he's talking about the séances again. 'But there was this time, we were all set up and waiting. There was a man with us, Jonathan, doesn't live in these parts now. At the time he were about thirty, full head of dark hair; a handsome man, some'd say. Anyway, we were all sitting there in silence when suddenly he closes his eyes, falls backwards and hits his head on the wall – then he sits forwards again and opens his eyes – but his face – it was different: a different expression, a different shape, his hair had gone grey around the temples, even his eyes had changed colour.'

John shakes his head as if he can't believe what he's

saying. 'He looked like he was trying to talk but all that came out was grunts and coughs, like a sicking dog. Then his eyes closed again and this time when they opened, he screamed and screamed and screamed – his face was his own, but now his hair had gone completely white.

'He had to go to hospital and it turned out his jaw was dislocated and his cheekbones had snapped, both of 'em, and he was bruised for weeks, poor sod. Something had changed the shape of his face, Edie, bent it to fit . . .'

'What happened to the rest of you?' I ask.

'Nowt,' says John, shaking his head. 'Jonathan moved away, like I said, not long afterwards. Mags was there. It hit her hard – she was already unwell, mind. And I've never been back to Newton Manor myself. But the important thing is, Edie, things happen around here, and you don't need to worry about me not believing, right, lass?'

'Right,' I say.

'So . . .' he says, expectantly.

'So?'

'So, what are you giving and who are you giving it to?'

'Nothing,' I say. 'I've always had visions, and that's all there is to it. I don't know what the fey are talking about and I suggest that you give them less credence, John Platt.'

He leans forward. 'It's a warning, Edie,' he says, 'and you can choose to ignore it or you can choose to act upon it, but I could not keep it from you. That's all there is to it.'

'Thank you for letting me know,' I say, standing up, 'and sorry if I'm being rude. I'm just very confused at the moment and I don't really know what to do about anything.'

'I know you're a good lass, Edie, so don't you worry yourself. I know you'll do the right thing, whatever it is.' He lets out a short, sharp laugh. 'I can't pretend to understand what the right thing is, myself, but I know you'll do it.'

'Thanks, John,' I say. 'Thanks for the tea, too.'

And then I turn and leave.

I park at Newton Manor, and walk the rest of the way in the rain. There's a general sense that the rain's not going to go away, that it's now something you have to just try and ignore if you want to get out at all.

And the dark circular patch is actually there, it really is there. I kneel down when I come to the edge of it. It's nearly as big as the stone circle itself: the edge of it nearly reaches the stones. The grass is not burnt, but it is different, thicker and waxier and longer. I pluck a blade and bring it to my face. It's a very dark green, and about as long and as wide as my finger. And weirdly, it doesn't look wet – and when I push my hands into the new grass, it's bone-dry. I stand on it and I can feel the rain on my skin, but it's like the ground is somehow immune.

For a time I stand there, looking at the stones, which somehow communicate with me, just through their appearance: how old they are, all of the different weathers they've experienced, the changes they've witnessed, and for this period of time in which I stand here on this strange grass and look at the stones, I feel as if I am outside time; I'm with them, the stones, in a place where the rules are different, where there is a great patience and sense of waiting. And there is also the sense that a change is coming, back in the human universe, where there is human life to feel it and see it and live through it – or not live through it, depending. Far away, in this world of the stones, I can hear wind that sounds like a voice or a voice that moans like the wind, and I can hear hissing and clicking and groaning sounds that are deeply inhuman in a way that is difficult to identify. These things are getting closer.

I close my eyes but I can still see the stones, towering over me, existing in a plane not delineated merely by our five human senses. I am beginning to realise this plane is a deeper, more fundamental reality, a world that the stones are connected to, somehow, a world that was perhaps once acknowledged by humankind, back when the stones were put in place, but has since been forgotten in quite a cold and deliberate way, a disdainful way – or maybe not forgotten, rather it has been strenuously denied. *When I became a man, I put away childish things.* What's that from, the Bible? What does it mean? Perhaps the stones and what-ever it is they represent have been disowned, *put away* – and after all, it is easy for people to forget things, as one generation and then the next slips on past . . .

I wish people could live for as long as stones.

I step out of the circle, out of both circles, the dark-grass circle and the stone circle. I pass between them and the rain is cold and wakes me up and I open my eyes and look around me and see the field again. I can hear the rain and the normal, earthly wind, and the sea, and seagulls. I can't hear the hissing and clicking and moaning and groaning any more. More than anything, the feeling is of *returning*. Like walking into your house after being outside in a storm. You come back in and close the door and feel safe again. That's what stepping out of the stone circle is like: coming home.

But I don't feel entirely safe, having said that. I feel like I can't quite close the door behind me, the dividing line between inside and outside is not quite thick enough, not quite strong enough to last.

I used to sleep in a huge bed when I lived with Grandma and Granddad. It was so soft and covered in blankets; I used to wonder if there was a mattress in there at all. I used to climb in between a different pair of blankets every night. It should have been uncomfortable, but it wasn't. I would sink into it. It was deep and giving. The quilt on top was always covered in a wine-red sheet. It was a feather quilt, and so old that all of the feathers stuck together at one end or one side, forming big thick lumps, while the rest of it remained thin. I think it even used to smell of dust, but

I'm not sure about that, maybe that's my memory adding details that weren't really there. Certainly, Grandma would always come in when I was a child and stick a hot water bottle under the quilt, whatever time of year it was, whatever the weather. She would often put the hot water bottle in between a different pair of blankets so that it would be merely a warm presence, something I could feel but not touch. There was an electric blanket too, I think, one of the old ones that were eventually recognised as a massive fire hazard.

Grandma used to tell me that my mum and her two sisters all slept in that bed together when they were children, and I used to imagine it and wonder what it would be like to have sisters. I still wonder that sometimes, even now.

The room around the bed was full of things that weren't really used any more. Before Grandma and Granddad took me in it had been a spare room and that's what it felt like, even when it became my room. Around the bed, piled up against the walls, there were old electric radios, boxes of crockery, chests of drawers full of bed linen and clothes – my mother's, and her sisters' too. There was even an old cot. There were toys that were not quite charming enough to have been given pride of place anywhere and yet they were, y'know, old toys, and so they had been kept here instead, not intentionally hidden away, but still.

There were framed pictures too, that had been taken

down to make room for others and never been put back up. There was a broken telephone, and household appliances that would not have looked out of place in a museum – things made out of that plastic that turns yellow over time: a whole history of old, yellowed, plastic things.

So I used to lie in this bed and wait to fall asleep in a way that I think of as childish although I have little experience of children and so I don't actually know if it is 'childish' at all. What I mean is, I used to lie in this huge bed with my eyes open, looking around the room and expecting sleep to just find me, somehow. And I'd look at the shadows thrown by the streetlight somewhere outside the window and find faces in the interplay between the shadows and the patterns of the embossed wallpaper. The same faces would be there every night and I used to look to them for reassurance, almost.

There were shadows and faces on the ceiling too, though they were smaller, because the ceiling was covered with spiky Artex.

There were faces in the curtains, but because the curtains were opened and closed every day, and ended up hanging differently every night, the faces in the curtains changed and I didn't find them reassuring at all.

One of the things that I liked best about that room – or the house, really – was that it was on a city street, not a busy one, but with occasional cars going past at odd hours of the night, and I really liked watching the patterns made on the ceiling by their headlights: the pale lines and bars and blocks, and the way they'd appear gently, and then slowly move across the ceiling from one side of the room to the other as the car passed by.

The sound of the cars was special too, although I didn't realise this until I was older. The sibilant hiss of a car at night, receding down the road away from your bedroom window; the sound of a car in the dark; or a motorcycle somewhere in the city during the night, driving away in the distance. The best is if you are trying to go to sleep and you are lying motionless in bed with your eyes closed and you hear a distant motorcycle and you listen to it intently, every last drop of its engine sound, without moving at all, without opening your eyes at all, and you can absorb it completely, beginning to end, that time it spends within earshot somehow physical, despite its distance, and you're just lying there, and it has been raining.

Though I do not live in the city any more.

I see Phillip sleeping alone in his double bed, sweating a lot and twitching, as if all his muscles are tightening and then relaxing. Sometimes he makes little whimpering sounds, the kind of sound somebody might make if they were lying curled up on the ground, anticipating a hard kick.

I see Phillip walking through Ravenglass, hands in pockets, his eyes on the estuary. I see him head between the houses of the main road towards the La'al Ratty, where he stands on a little bridge that traverses the narrow-gauge railway and looks down at all of the tourists boarding the tiny train. He takes his camera from a pocket and starts taking photographs.

I see Phillip masturbating in front of his computer, frequently. I see photos and videos of women undressing or showering: images that often have half of the subject out of frame so that the women are truncated in various ways. I see Phillip standing in the shower for a long, long time, not washing himself. I see Phillip receiving a delivery of a stack of newspapers. He gets all of the newspapers, every day, delivered.

CHAPTER FOURTEEN

I catch myself standing in the kitchen with my sleeve rolled up, picking at the bandage on my arm. I lift one edge up and have a good look at the cut. It has still not had a chance to scab properly or heal, but beneath the gauze the blood is dry. The lips of the wound look to be almost healing themselves, rounding off somehow, skinning over. They're becoming two little ridges, like real lips, and they're itchy.

I jump as Mitchell enters the kitchen behind me and yank the sleeve down. 'You're early,' I say.

'I'm not,' he says. 'I'm late. Get with the programme, boss.'

I look at him, and he holds his wrist up and taps his watch. He's right.

I nod. 'You're late, bitch,' I say. 'Get down and give me twenty.'

*   *   *

The strange discoloration has spread now so that almost as soon as I enter the field in which the Greycroft stones stand I unwittingly walk onto darker, thicker grass, and I can hear those inhuman sounds, the hissing and clicking and mournful wind-voice. I scurry backwards, back off the dark grass. The stones are on the other side of the field and I cannot get close to them without crossing this weird new field, because that's how I think of it: a new field laid across the top of the old one, or risen up through the old one.

From here the stones look taller and sharper than I thought they were, and perhaps more regular in their shape. They are changing. The whole place is changing – and the change is spreading, unfolding outwards from here.

I should speak to the Candle, because of course it is something to do with the Candle, itself something to do with me.

I look at the stones and they are so regular and sharp and evenly spaced now, like the top of a crown, perhaps, as if there is a great dead giant queen or king buried underneath, but on their feet and not their back.

One night, when I'm driving my can't-sleep drive, I head north on the A595, which is the direction I normally take, but instead of turning off into the valleys, I keep on going, letting the car pick up speed, making the most of the wider, flatter, straighter road. I don't have a destination in mind and I don't know what time it is, though there's a lightness in the sky that suggests it is way past midnight, past the earliest of the early hours, perhaps about four or five o'clock.

I drive through the Seascale-Gosforth crossroads and keep going, passing through Calder Bridge and Ponsonby. I think about turning off to Beckermet and St Bees and Nethertown to see the houses on the beach, but the A595 holds me to it like a magnet. When I get to Egremont, I eschew the bypass for the main street and look at the charity shops, bakeries and pubs to see which ones have closed or opened or been replaced since the last time I was here. I pass by the statues of miners at the school gates and look briefly up at the sixties tower block that presides over the whole town like a squat god. The tower block is part of the school; it's where they teach science. Mitchell has told me about the rooms full of old, thick wooden workbenches with gas taps for the Bunsen burners the kids use to burn their notebooks, and tanks of little fish that the boys dare each other to swallow alive.

At the end of the main street another roundabout spits me back out onto the A595 and I carry on to Whitehaven.

The supermarket is open already – it is probably open twenty-four hours a day. I slow down and turn into the car park just as the sun begins to rise. Big rectangular boards advising petrol prices tower up blackly against the vivid pinkness of the sky. I drive across the car park diagonally, enjoying the absence of other cars, and choose a parking space near the entrance. The impression that I get from others is that a parking space near the entrance of the supermarket is a rare thing, usually, a rare treat to be seized, to be celebrated.

I sit in the car and look at the building's door, a yellow square, and then twist around and look at the sky through the rear windscreen. I open the door, get out of the car and walk round to the back, and, leaning against it, I put my hands in my pockets. I feel like I am living in the future and the future is all giant empty car parks and empty twenty-four-hour supermarkets and pink skies and silhouettes. The future is a perpetual dimness, a perpetual pre-dawn light, and everybody in it is driving.

If I'd been asleep, the banging on my door would have woken me, but as it happens I was not asleep. I get out of bed and put my dressing gown on.

'Edie!' somebody hisses.

'Who is it?'

'It's John!'

With the hissing, I'm not sure which John it is. I open the door to find it's Senior, which I'm relieved about. He's wearing wellies, waterproof trousers and a long oilskin.

'What are you dressed for?' I ask.

'We've got to go,' he says, gesturing with a massive old torch. 'The fey have told me where to go, to find it.'

'To find what?'

'The bad thing,' he says, 'whatever it is. Come on, lass, get your things together.'

'The fey? Do you believe them?'

'Yes, I bloody believe 'em: they're scared, Edie, and they want us to fix things.'

'And where do we go?'

'Newton Manor. Where the magic always was.'

'We should wait until morning.' I don't want John to know about the Candle or any of this until I've got Phillip sorted; if I don't find what I need to prove what he's done, then people will continue to suspect Gabe.

'They're right frit.'

'Jesus,' I say. On the other hand, he can't think I'm hiding anything, or he might go on his own. 'All right, then. But I don't know what you expect to find.'

We stand before Newton Manor in the pouring rain. I know the Candle is inside; upstairs, I think. I focus on forming the words *stay where you are* in my mind and beaming them up to it. That's how I visualise it: a beam of light shooting from my head to an upstairs window. *Hide.* I'm wearing wellies and my dull waterproof jacket, which is zipped up to my nose. I wish I had an oilskin.

'We used to use the front door,' he says, gesturing at the padlock.

'We still could, I reckon.' I examine the door. 'The padlock's solid but the bracket is loose and the wood's cracked around it. Looks like someone's tried to crowbar it off.' I stand back and then aim one swift, hard kick at the edge of the door. The wood around the bracket splits further. The sound would be loud and abrasive, but it is masked by the heavy rain. I kick it again and again, and by the time the bracket comes off with the padlock, I'm out of breath.

We watch as the door swings inwards, then I look at John, who shuffles forward and walks through the door. 'Wish I could still kick things,' he says as he passes. 'Can't do much more with me legs than walk these days.'

The hallway is almost pitch-black and my eyes have to adjust. I suspect it would be dim anyway, because it's quite narrow and the only window that lets onto this space is small, but as it's night, it's even darker. The window is at the top of the first flight of stairs up ahead. It's slightly open – that must be the window I looked through last time I came here.

All I can hear is the wind, making a strange fluting sound through the open window, and a ceaseless dripping. At first I wonder where the dripping is coming from, but then I see what little light there is reflecting off the water running in rivulets down the wall. My foot lands in a puddle and I realise that the dripping is everywhere; the black and white tiles of the floor are covered in water and droplets are falling from the ceiling.

The floral wallpaper is – or was – pale green, with some pattern I can't make out repeated across it. It is slack and bubbly now and I imagine that further in, hidden by the darkness, it's peeling off the walls.

The Candle is definitely upstairs. I can't hear it, but I can feel it burning. The bright light over the seascape of my consciousness. Again, I will the words *don't move.*

'It's a bit grim,' I say.

'It used to be beautiful,' John says sadly. 'It's a right shame to see it like this. It was old Mrs Bretton's pride and joy, it was.'

I move further in and my foot collides with something. There's a loud, metallic clatter and whatever it is bounces forwards and ricochets off the skirting board. '*Shit!*' I say, then, 'Shit! It's cans – some empty beer cans, that's all. Sorry.'

'This is going to finish me off,' John says, a hand on his chest. 'I can feel it.'

'Don't say that.'

'Here,' John says, and a beam of light appears. 'I've got a torch.' As he shines it around the hallway I remember that I've got one too: a little one on my keyring. There are three doorways leading from the hall; only one actually has a door in it. To the left of the staircase are more stairs, going down. These are sandstone steps, and as we get closer I can see each one is worn in the middle.

'What's that?' I ask as John sweeps the room with the torch. 'Point it at the banisters. There was something hanging down.'

When John does, I see there are a few long, thin white things hanging from the wooden rail. They look like slime, or alien chrysalides, or strips of skin, or melting fat. I don't dare approach them until suddenly I realise what they are. 'Oh.' I turn back to John. 'Condoms.'

'Kids,' he says, and briefly points the torch down at the empty cans. It also picks out an old pizza box, turned to mush by the wet.

Water is trickling down the stone staircase and gathering in the hollows of each step. Over time the flow will carve out its own channel. The ceiling feels low. The stairwell is very dark indeed. The same wallpaper has been used down here, but it's peeling badly and the walls are much more mouldy. There's a bad smell, like something rotting, and when something creaks higher up in the house I feel as if a balloon has suddenly inflated in my stomach.

'What was that?' I whisper.

'Probably just the building,' John says, 'shifting, like. In the wet.'

We carry on down the steps, following them as they turn so we're heading back towards the front door, but below ground. My heart is bouncing around inside my chest. 'This was a bad idea,' I say. 'We shouldn't have come here.'

'I think we should have,' John murmurs. 'Look at these walls.'

'What do you mean?'

'The wallpaper's been scraped off – look, here. Something big has come down here.'

'Let's go.'

'No.' He puts a hand on my shoulder. 'Nobody is going to sort this out if we don't.'

'Why can't we just go to the police and tell them everything?'

'Tell them what, exactly? What do we know? Trust me on this, Edie. It's up to us. We have to find out what's happening.'

I look back at the walls. In the light of our torches I can see wavy dark-brown smears roughly following the angle of the stairs. It's blood, I think, with what looks like matted hair stuck in amongst it in places, on both sides of the wall. It looks like whatever it was had to squeeze itself down.

I try to keep a lid on things and follow John into the cellar, which is a couple of inches deep in water. In the light from the torches we can see the rough walls are white-washed, but the lime has flaked off in great chunks, exposing irregularly-shaped cobbles beneath. Apart from—

'Why is there a shower down here?' I ask, pointing my little LED torch off to the right. 'See that?'

Through a wide archway there's a separate room that's actually a bathroom; the walls are covered in dark blue mosaic tiles, though the grout is dark with fungus. A heavily oxidised old metal bracket protrudes from one wall, supporting the showerhead I saw. A long black string hangs from the head – some kind of algae, maybe, or a type of mildew.

'The wet room,' says John. He sounds wistful.

I look at him.

'Let's just say the parties were wild.' He turns away. 'Truth be told, it was always a bit horrible, like. There was cracks in t'grout and bugs would get in. Big earwigs, mostly.'

I look back at the shower. It looks like a reptilian creature: a metallic spitting cobra balanced on its tail. I imagine the space well-lit, fully tiled, the shower running and steam rising, maybe a large bath inset into the ground, and naked people kissing, writhing, fucking, maybe somebody chanting. It sounds like they were all pretending to be Romans. I picture earwigs running around. The earwigs are probably still here.

Another empty doorway opens onto darkness. I follow John as he disappears into it. The torch picks out the uneven texture of the walls which are just earth here. The passage rises slightly and the ground is not so wet. Bloody streaks mark the walls again, but when I point them out to John he just nods and points his torch at the ground.

There are hoofprints – not regularly spaced, but all over the place, and they're coupled with long gouges, as if the animal was being dragged through the mud.

'A horse?' I say. My voice is flat in the tunnel.

'Looks like it,' John says. 'Though I don't know what state

it was in. They must have forced it down those stairs back there; it couldn't have walked.'

'And it was bleeding.'

We walk in silence. The passage continues to rise, and occasionally it bends quite sharply. Then it starts dropping again. After a while I've lost track of where we are and how long we've been walking. It's stuffy and warm and the rotting smell is stronger here.

I can hear a faint buzzing sound. 'That's flies,' I say.

'Nearly there,' John says, and shortly afterwards, the passage opens up into a dome-shaped chamber. There's another passage leading off it.

'Jesus Christ,' I say.

'Hell,' John says. '*Hell.*'

By the torchlight we can see the edge of a pit that's been dug in the ground. It's half-full of some kind of thick, bloody soup. Above it the huge, long face of a great chestnut horse looms from the shadows and stares back at us. But the face is disfigured. It's hard to tell, but the horse must have been arranged in a kneeling position in the liquid. Its head is almost detached, so vicious are the wounds in the back of its neck. Great chunks of flesh have been removed from its flanks – the cuts are so deep in places that I can see its ribs. Its eyes have been removed and its tongue cut out. It's got two deep wounds in its back, near the bottom of its neck, as if it had wings that have been dug out.

I walk around the pit. It looks like the wound's been

made with a blade. Flies crawl over the body and settle on the surface of the slop it's lying in.

For a brief moment I see the horse alive, screaming and thrashing around in this little room, knocking lit candles onto the floor, its mouth foaming, drool running from between its huge teeth. I see a knife go into its neck; I see the blood run free. And that blood is so very bright; so very rich. I want to put my hands into that cascade; I want to taste it. I—

The beam of light from John's torch is shivering.

I can see candles in the numerous small alcoves in the walls of the chamber. There is an ancient, ramshackle desk collapsing against one wall and a couple of knackered-looking cabinets with their doors hanging off by the hinges.

John hasn't moved from the passageway.

'What do you make of this?' I ask him. 'Is horse sacrifice something else you used to do?'

He shakes his head. His mouth open, he doesn't look at me, just at the horse.

'Have you ever heard of it?' I ask.

He blinks and closes his mouth and clears his throat and shakes his head again.

'We can work it out later.' He turns around, back to the horse. 'Come on, lass; let's get away from this place.'

We turn and run.

CHAPTER FIFTEEN

The first thing I do after getting back to the caravan is turn on the laptop and then Google 'horse sacrifice'. The first result is a Wikipedia entry with 'Horse Sacrifice' as an actual title; it describes various horse sacrifice rites from around the world, but the most interesting is one recorded by Geraldus Cambrensis.

There is, in a northern and remote part of Ulster, among the Kenelcuni, a certain tribe which is wont to install a king over itself by an excessively savage and abominable ritual. In the presence of all the people of this land in one place, a white mare is brought into their midst. Thereupon he who is to be elevated, not to a prince but to a beast, not to a king but to an outlaw, steps forward in beastly fashion and exhibits his bestiality. Right thereafter the mare is killed and boiled piecemeal in water, and in the same water a bath is prepared for him. He gets into the bath and eats of the flesh that is brought to him, with his people standing around and sharing it with him. He also imbibes the broth in which he is bathed, not from any vessel, nor with his hand, but only with his mouth. When this is done right according to such unrighteous ritual, his rule and sovereignty are consecrated.

I also read about Geraldus himself: Gerald of Wales. There is some suggestion that, as a mediaeval clergyman, his records of Celtic culture are not to be taken at face value because he had a vested interest in painting an unpleasant picture of Celtic society in order to foment a prejudice advantageous to his own faith and his own culture.

But still, thinking about the ritual piques my own morbid curiosity. I close the laptop and imagine it: 'He who is to be elevated, not to a prince but to a beast, steps forward in beastly fashion and exhibits his bestiality.' Maybe the horse beneath Newton Manor was killed in order to aid someone's elevation, or . . . or maybe it was the Candle, and the Candle sacrificed the horse in memory of its own elevation, if the Candle was a human being once. I know very little of the Candle, but I can imagine it being the result of some kind of magic, magic that secures 'elevation', perhaps; is elevation immortality?

I can imagine the ritual itself; I can imagine being that man, he who is to be elevated. I imagine it happening around here and my mind settles on Irton Pike; a low summit at the near end of Wasdale.

My people are crowded on the slopes of the Pike, lit only by the lights from the fires. Some of the flames have broken loose and ignited the heather; one hillside is completely aflame. My people are howling and drinking, dancing and fighting. I am seated at the peak on a throne of wood. Before me is a platform on which to stand, also wooden, and a gigantic bronze cauldron filled with boiling water. It is suspended in a firepit, the top of it level with the earth. The sky is clear and full of stars. I have starved myself for three days, before which I attempted to stretch my stomach by gorging myself. I am waiting. I am too excited to join my people in their celebrating. They are staying away from me. Beneath my cloak I massage my manhood into a full erection.

There is a roar from those tribesmen at the bottom of the slope and I catch a glimpse of something large and orange in the firelight. By the sun it would be white. It is the mare. I watch as they drag her up the hill.

She cries out, and I cry out, 'Don't hurt her!' I stand up and everybody falls silent. 'Don't hurt her!' I shout, again. 'She is for me!' My body is weak and feels strange; my tattoos hang loose. My voice is rough. My people look at me, something feral in their faces. *Fear*: the admiration one animal feels for a stronger animal.

They bring the mare to me. She is wet with foam and sweat by the time she has reached the top. My subjects have stopped wailing and cavorting. The silence is broken only by the panting of the mare and the faint whispering of the breeze in the treetops that surround this little mountain.

I step down from my throne and raise my arms and the crowd responds with a mighty cheer. My strongest men move the mare around so she is standing between the throne and the cauldron with her nose to the water. She does not protest. I move behind her and drop my cloak. I step up onto the platform. My erection is red and aching.

I thrust it into the mare's cunt and she whinnies and snorts. My men hold her steady and the crowd chants in time with my motions.

I dig my fingers into her haunches. Sweat is running into my eyes and I close them and lean into the horse. *Back and forth and back and forth.* I don't know how long it takes. I resist the urge to fantasise. I have to know what it is that I do.

When I am finished I withdraw and step around to let my people see that it is done. I take a knife from one of the men holding the mare in place and I cut her throat. She bleeds into the water and falls over. The water is red now. The mare screams again and thrashes around on the ground, one hoof splashing the water all over me. The pain is distant. Everybody is watching in silence. My skin feels hot. The red water runs down over me. I put the knife in through her eye and hold it there until she stops moving.

My men move forward and start cutting into her, removing hunks of flesh and throwing them into the steaming water. They pull out her internal organs and throw those in too, and flay the skin into strips. Everything goes in apart from the bones, which are left, held together by tendons and ligaments, on the rocks by the cauldron. By now the water is boiling, and thickening as blood, piss, whatever was in the mare's stomach, bladder and bowels starts cooking. I grab a piece of flesh from the surface and examine it. At my gesture one of the men kicks out the fire beneath the cauldron.

I hold out my hands and someone ties my wrists together. We wait, and when the water is no longer hot enough to kill me they lift me over the side and lower me in. I sit with my back to the stinging metal, and it sears the skin over my spine. The sludgy broth presses in, and I lower my mouth to the liquid and start to drink. It is gritty and tastes burnt. When something too large to swallow arrives at my mouth, I have to eat it, chewing it into pieces without using my hands. I have to consume every last morsel: all the meat; all the liquor. I slurp and sip, I chew and swallow and chew again until I am as full as a pig and retching with each mouthful. I have seen men die engaged in this feat, choking on their own vomit or climbing from the cauldron and writhing upon the rocky ground, clutching at their grotesquely distended bellies as their stomachs split and poison their blood.

And this *is* a feat; an act strange and deliberate enough to attract the attention of the monsters that govern this universe. Everything is built upon blood. Our history is a tower with its foundations mired in blood. Everything anybody pays for was once killed for; all ownership has its roots in murder and the sowing of fear. This is a ritual to demonstrate understanding of the cruel mechanics of our world, and all of the worlds beside it, and it will be rewarded.

The eating takes me the rest of the night and the following day and I don't finish until the sun is setting, but I do finish it. I am sick and ill and spouting filth by the end, but I do it, though I can barely move. I am bloated like a long-dead thing.

My people are still with me. The fires are still burning. There is no heather or bracken left on this hilltop now, only ash and smoke and the stripped bones of animals that have been killed and roasted and consumed. The sky is spanned by strips of black cloud, between which can be seen the furious red and orange sunset; the sun is a livid welt disappearing into the bloody sea. For a moment I know that Hell is like this, and I know that I have succeeded: the world has touched me and I have been found. I am *elevated*. I am no longer human. I am demonic.

I slowly rise to my feet in the empty cauldron, breathing deeply. I feel as if I could just softly break open. I am covered in stinking, congealing fluids: the mare's and my own. My people are silent, waiting, and I raise both hands to the sky and roar, and my voice is not my own any more. My people roar back, and from the trees around the base of the Pike an army of great black birds rises screaming into the sky.

That's how I imagine it. That's how I would have done it.

I close the laptop and look around me and at all of my things, my possessions, the interior of my tiny home. I try hard not to cry. I feel distracted, and I can't stop thinking about horses, and I don't know what to do. I don't know what I can do that will matter, that will be important, that will be worth doing.

It starts as drizzle and builds into heavy rain and then remains, more constant than weather should be: steady, relentless and unbending. It batters the leaves and the windows; it creeps in beneath the doorways. It runs playfully down the sides of the road and leaks through roofs with malice. It fills the river and muddies up the estuary.

I'm beneath the trees, where the rain has become great big globules that fall slowly to the ground, more slowly than the rain falls out in the open, and more sparsely too, funnelled together by the branches overhead. My wellies slop through the almost-liquid layer of dead brown leaves. I want to see how John is doing after last night, and tell him what I read about horse sacrifices.

Once I am through the trees I am subjected to the downpour in earnest. The short route over the fellside turns into a trudge over spongy scrub that hides deep mud and surface water. There are no views; just the pressing-in of pale, opaque sky.

I can hear sheep baa-ing on the mountain. I always notice livestock sounds – the lowing and braying and strange pained shouting – are louder when it's dark, ringing out across the fields and the valleys and the rivers and the woodland.

When I get to the farm I feel straight away that it is

different, although I cannot see exactly how. Then I realise the windows have been boarded up. The farmhouse doesn't have shutters like The Tup; these are actual boards, nailed on.

I wonder if they've boarded up the windows because of the rain? But no, of course not; that doesn't make sense. It's as dark as night, almost.

I knock on the door and go to open it, but the door that's always open is locked. I try again, just to make sure, and the handle turns easily, properly, but the door doesn't open. It's definitely locked. I step back and look again at the boarded windows. They've used planks of wood pulled from pallets and old bits of plywood from I don't know where. I knock on the door harder, repeatedly, not stopping.

The rain remains totally constant: no wind, no diminishing, no sudden intensification.

I keep knocking until there's a sudden screeching sound from inside and then I stop. I hear one of them shout something incoherent, and then footsteps come towards the door.

'What do you want?' It's John Junior. He yanks open the door just wide enough for me to see his face.

I wait for him to ask me in, or at least step aside, but he doesn't.

'Is your dad here?' I ask.

'He is, but you're not seeing him. What the hell do you think you're doing, coming here and asking him all these questions about Mum?' He opens the door a little wider.

'Not to mention encouraging all this shite about fairies? And taking him to Newton Manor with you? He's an old man, Edie!'

'He's completely with it,' I say. 'Don't talk about him like he's incapable or like he's mad.'

'Then why does he keep babbling about some fucking bad thing coming? Why do I keep finding him crying over pictures of Mum, or standing there in the middle of the room with a great big fuck-off hard-on, staring down at it like he doesn't know what it is? Why did he spend all last night hammering boards over the windows "to keep the angry little lasses out"?'

'Sounds like you've answered your own question there.'

'And what the fuck is it with you being so goddamn calm about everything?' He steps forwards and jabs a finger at me. 'Making jokes like nothing's wrong? My dad's a wreck, he's completely fucking lost it, and it's your fault, Edie! And you just stand there with your yellow fucking wellies on and say – what, what was it? "Sounds like you've answered your own question there"? Well, yeah, thank you very much for that, very fucking helpful. Very remorseful.'

He stares at me and he's far enough out of the doorway to be getting rained on himself now, and the water courses down his forehead and drips from his thick eyebrows and hangs, suspended, in the tangle of his beard.

'Look,' I say, 'you should give your dad more credit. Don't dismiss everything—'

'I'm *not* dismissing him! I'm *worried* about him! I'm worried that you, with your weird questions and your weird obsession with Mum and your weird pleasure at his – his delusions, have really upset him. I'm worried that you've done something to him. I'm not *angry* with him; I'm angry with *you*. To think what I did for you. To think I felt enough to–'

He stops talking abruptly and puts a hand to his forehead.

'What?' I say.

'You know how I know it's all nonsense?' he asks. 'You know why I don't really believe him when he talks about something bad coming, or about the fairies?'

'How?'

'Because I did believe it. I *did*. I believed it so much that I tried to use it – I tried magic. And it didn't fucking work, did it?'

I look at him. He just looks back. Somehow he is not blinking despite the rain.

'What do you mean?' I ask.

'Girt,' he hisses, and when I shake my head, still not getting it, he says, 'For you. It was a love spell, for you. I needed sacrifice; I needed blood, and she was just here, just . . . She was getting old anyway, and I just thought . . . I thought it would work.' He bites his lip. 'But it *didn't* work. It didn't work, did it?'

'No,' I say. 'It didn't work. You must have done it wrong.'

214

'Or maybe it's all fucking bollocks!' he shouts. 'All those old books? I spent so long going through all those dusty old books at night after he'd gone to bed, all those old fucking cookbooks and almanacs and journals and local histories and spell books, and it's all absolute bollocks.'

'If it's any consolation,' I say, 'I don't want to fall in love, not with anyone. So it would have been a kind of coercion – it would have been a trick. You would have cheated me into your life, into your bed.'

He doesn't say anything but looks down at the ground for a moment.

'Why didn't you just try things the normal way?' I ask. 'Talking to me a bit more? Being around a bit more? Letting me get to know you?'

'I knew you weren't really interested in anybody that way, Edie. We both know that the normal ways wouldn't have worked with you. You more or less just said it.'

'So that makes it okay to force me?'

He doesn't reply.

'I'll try another question, then.' I'm raising my voice now. 'Why me, if you knew I wasn't interested?'

His face hardens. 'Who else?'

'If either of us have hurt your father, John, it's you and what you did to Girt. You're a disgrace.'

He opens his mouth to respond, but then closes it again. Just before he slams the door I hear a sound from deeper within the farmhouse: a wail, a sob. It continues after the door is closed, a muffled howling behind and beneath the sound of the rain.

All of the doorways around the yard look so black. The clouds in the sky move like creatures migrating, getting away. A gate keeps banging somewhere in the darkness and something flaps across the yard, making me jump. It's nothing, some black plastic sheeting, torn loose by the wind. I can hear things moving in the shadows: wood creaking, metal clanking.

On my way back to The Tup I think about his final words. *Who else?* It is a valid point – there are not many single women around here of an age suitable for John Junior. Not that that's an excuse, obviously. He might have said it only in order to hurt my feelings, but there's probably some truth in it.

I grow to love the passion I can hear when the Candle comes for my blood: the base, unthinking desperation in the sound; the pleasure in the slaking of the urge. It is simple and vibrant, whereas the rest of the world is becoming grey and confused. I still don't know what my blood does for it, but that doesn't matter to me. I lie in my bed and listen to the groaning and the slurping and I feel a smile come to my lips and a glow settles in my stomach. Maybe this is how it feels to have a pet, or to satisfy somebody sexually? Sometimes, when the Candle calls, I run my finger around my belly button and trail my hand across my abdomen and as the tingling spreads across my skin I slowly move my hand down and touch myself between the legs. My other hand moves to my breast and I find my heart beating quicker and my nipples tightening as I listen to the grunts coming from beneath me and my head fills with the sound of other people's laughter, which is something that becomes ever more arousing – or maybe the Candle chooses more sensual voices, lower voices, throatier laughter, more understated, sometimes interwoven with the gasps of orgasm. It is increasingly so, actually, and now a vision will come and I'll see figures moving in a darkened room, bedclothes falling back, a woman on top, the lips of her pussy and the shaft of the man's cock wet with her secretions, reflecting light. The detail of their fucking is the only bright thing in the room. The brightness brings to mind an image that I can't immediately place – colourful, living apples hanging in a dead-looking orchard.

The best thing is that I know it is happening, I know it is really happening, right at the same time as I am lying here: these two are really fucking, really kissing, really moaning, and I can see it all and hear it all, and they don't know I'm watching.

It is best when I don't know who they are.

I see Phillip slowly undress and stand naked in front of the mirror and cup his saggy belly in his hands and tweak his nipples despondently. He runs his fingers through his chest hair and holds it at full length and looks down at it. He examines his hairline. He turns around and looks over his shoulder at his own buttocks and then turns back, so that he's facing the mirror again. He looks sad, then angry, and then he almost storms away, like he's just had an argument with his reflection.

I see Phillip rooting through the shoeboxes that are stacked up at the top of his wardrobe. I see him take photo wallets out of the shoeboxes; they are bright green or bright yellow or bright blue and they all bear the logos and names of now-defunct film-processing companies. He takes photos out of the wallets, sits on the bed and starts looking through them. I see more photos of women and teenage girls. All of the photos have the same surreptitiously-caught sensibility, that taken-from-a-hidden-place look – actually, I come to realise not quite all of them are like that. There are some pictures of a girl who is looking directly at the camera; it is impossible for her not to have known that the photos were being taken. The first shows only her face, and she does not look happy. She has something covering her mouth. The next photo shows her whole naked body, with her arms behind her. Her ankles are bound. Phillip looks at this picture for a long time. Then he looks at the next one, which is similar, except the girl is clearly under water. She is submerged and the water is kind of murky, so her body is just a pale shape, really.

I see Phillip walking in the dark over the great big lattice bridge that crosses the estuary. He has a bag in his hand. He descends the steps at the far side, the north side and makes his way to the water's edge. The tide is in tonight. He starts throwing the contents of the bag into the water and I see that the small things he's throwing are pink little prawns. Then my vision zooms in and I don't know what I'm seeing – whether it's something actually under the water, or something that Phillip is imagining or remembering. I see a mass of boiling black that at first looks like oil, but then I realise it isn't, and it isn't actually boiling, it's a knot of eels thrashing around underwater. Occasionally a round eye flashes past my field of vision and an open mouth with a few sharp, spiny teeth becomes briefly visible.

Chapter Sixteen

The next night I put the blood under the caravan and then leave the door open just a crack so I can watch the Candle come and get it. But it's a dark and cloudy night and when the Candle gets close – which I both hear and feel, inside me – I still don't really *see* it. I see *something*, moving towards me, but it brings the shadows with it, stretching them out or making them swell up, and I find it hard to focus on anything. When I look right at it – the clump of darkness, I mean – I wonder if I can see it at all, and then, when I look somewhere else, I see it moving again, out of the corner of my eye. Its movement is smooth and fluid, but I can hear a squelching sound, like I did that first night the Candle came to me. It stops by the back door of The Tup, a black mass diffusing.

'What is the Elsewhere?' I whisper.

There is a moment of silence, then a growing murmur as the Candle assembles the voices it requires.

A vast place of much variety. There are worlds upon worlds out there. Imagine a great house of long corridors and an infinite number of rooms, and each room is a different plane, a different dimension, a different kind of existence.

'I feel like I've always lived in somebody else's house,' I say. 'I've always been a guest, not at home.'

The Earth is nobody's home. The Earth is the entrance to the Elsewhere; nothing more, nothing less. You cannot enter that great and beautiful house without first crossing the threshold. Earth is that threshold. Every spirit that ever found the Elsewhere came through life here on Earth. You have never felt at home here because you have the Eye; you have always known, on some level, that there is more to life and to being than this one planet.

'It's the afterlife?'

Parts of it receive your dead, yes. But not all spirits get to roam the whole entirety; for that you have to take certain measures.

'Like you did.'

Yes.

'What do you want with here, then? Why have you come back?'

This was my land once. It was taken from me and they burned my body on that field overlooking the sea. I want it back. And then I want to keep the gates to the Elsewhere. I want to manage the threshold. I want the power.

'Would I be at home in the Elsewhere?'

Yes.

'You'll take me there?'

It is bleeding through, as we speak. You've seen it at the stones, where they left my ashes.

'And will I go there when I die?'

Edie, I need the blood.

'It's here,' I say, gesturing. 'Come and get it. I want to see what you look like.'

Silence, a heavy silence, and then the whispering voices suddenly rise in pitch and scream, briefly, all of them at once, and it's horrible. I recoil and find myself sitting on the top step of the caravan, my hands firmly over my ears.

You do not want to see what I look like, Edie.

'I do,' I say.

No, you don't. Take my word.

The hedgerows and drystone walls speed into and out of my little island of light and the night remains black and impenetrable outside it. Sometimes I feel that it's only my headlights that call the world into being; and before that happens, there isn't actually anything there at all. The road and the bright white raindrops and the grey walls don't exist at all until I perceive them, and at that moment of perception, or just before it, the universe or some other power or energy decides, somehow, exactly what is going to appear that that moment: that moment of illumination.

The Candle gives me hope, in a very real and meaningful

way - hope of other, better worlds beyond this one. I suppose that is what candles are supposed to do. But it does seem to be a hopeful thing, some entity arriving from somewhere else; a definite, concrete sign that we are not alone, that our lives are not the be all and end all. And to help it stay here – it's as if I'm harbouring an alien, like the little boy in *E.T.* It's an honour, an obligation. It's something worthwhile to do.

CHAPTER SEVENTEEN

I get the tray of eggs out of the walk-in fridge and manage to drop it before even getting as far as the morning-clean worktop. The tray lands upside down, of course, and the impact sounds like the crushing of a very large snail. I stand and look down at the mess as the yolks ooze out and spread across the floor and I can't move, I can't think of what to do. Is this all of the eggs? It can't be. What will I do for the contractors? Part of me just wants to get down on my hands and knees and press my face into the yolk, lick up the fragments of shell, lose myself in the rawness of it just for a moment.

I go back to the fridge. There are another three trays of eggs. Of course there are. There are always so many trays. But it's only when I see them that I know this. Before I saw them, I didn't know anything. I couldn't remember. I still am not sure how to go about cleaning this up, or if getting on with the cooking is more important.

I can't think about anything.

'Edie,' Maria says on Thursday night as I'm leaving the bar, heading through the doorway into the kitchen, 'the day after tomorrow is the bonfire. You haven't forgotten?'

'No,' I say, though I had forgotten, actually. Today, much like yesterday, has been lived in a half-light. I have seen everything as if from behind bevelled glass. Real life, my own life, is paling away against the visions, the stones, the Candle.

'And are you sure you can manage?' Maria asks.

'Yes,' I say, 'I'm feeling okay, thank you.'

'Are you going to go to the doctor's?'

'No. No, I'm feeling better.'

'Good. Jason Bull is going to do the fire and the fire-works – I would've asked one of the Johns Platt but they haven't been around so much. Did anything happen with you and John, by the way?'

'What? What do you mean?'

'You know! *John* . . . he asked you out for a walk, didn't he?' Maria looks at me expectantly. I don't say anything and she presses further. 'Well? Have you done anything with him?'

'Oh,' I reply, 'no, no I haven't. Yeah, he hasn't been in recently, has he?'

'I thought maybe he had embarrassed himself.'

I shake my head. I'd forgotten about John's kiss, but won't mention it. I don't want to get into all of that now.

'Nothing happened between us. Nothing at all.'

'Did you want it to?' Maria's initial snappiness has gone, giving way to her curiosity, her prurience.

'Not really,' I say. 'I don't really want a relationship.'

She purses her lips. 'Do you have any plans for your life, Edie?'

'No,' I say, 'no, I don't – but even if I did, a relationship wouldn't be amongst them. I just don't want one, Maria. I want to be on my own for as long as I can look after myself, and then I want to die quickly and unwittingly.' I said all that without thinking; it is true, but I didn't mean to say it. Like I say, my body, my mouth, they're all working on automatic at the moment.

I don't think Maria knows what to say. Why would she?

'Sorry,' I say. 'I'm just tired. Goodnight, Maria.' I slip through the doorway, through the darkened kitchen with all its metal edges gleaming in the light from the bar. It's early November and my breath is already misting. The stars are out in force tonight, sharp and bright in the clear sky.

The trees around the garden are bare and the leaves underfoot are crisp with the night frost. I light a cigarette and inhale. My hands are trembling.

We don't open the pub on Saturday because we're preparing for the bonfire – though Maria's preparations take the form of carving a pumpkin into something horrendously intricate for the pumpkin competition she's decided to hold.

She's doing it on the bar, which is covered with old newspapers, and pumpkin flesh and seeds are going everywhere.

'That'll take you all day,' I say.

'Yes,' she says, 'that's what it takes to win: time and effort.'

'I've got three hundred Cumberland sausages for hotdogs,' I say. 'I'm going to do a chunky vegetable soup for the vegetarians. Do you reckon that'll be enough?'

'Enough savoury, yes.'

'I'm doing black toffee and toffee-apples as well.'

'All sounds excellent,' Maria says. She looks up from the pumpkin, which is huge. 'Thank you, Edie.'

'I'm going to get chopping onions. Who's judging this pumpkin competition, anyway?'

'Mrs Cook.'

'Is Gabe going to be around later? It would be a shame for him to miss it – to feel like he can't come.'

'He'll be there.' Maria gestures with the tablespoon she's holding. 'Trust me.'

Jason and Gabe are out on the estuary building the fire. People have been dropping off their rubbish for it: garden clippings, old furniture, cardboard boxes. It looks like it's going to be pretty massive.

When I was a child there was a pub near my grandparents' house that did a big bonfire every November. It was one of my favourite nights of the year. The fire was always huge, and we'd see it get built up in the days leading up to the night itself. Like the one Jason and Gabe are building, it was mostly a big mound of stuff nobody wanted any more with a dense wooden core – pallets, windblown branches, broken kitchen chairs, that kind of thing. I think they used to stick a bale of hay in the middle as well.

I watch the two small figures on the sand from the pub doorway: one little stickman handing things to the other, who's standing on top of the pile itself. Jason will be setting the fireworks up on the grassy banks there.

All I can hear is the surf as the tide goes out.

By the time seven o'clock rolls around, the pub is the busiest it's been since the night Phillip was barred. People are laughing, clinking glasses, talking to people they haven't seen for a long time. There are people here from Gosforth, Seascale, the valleys, Egremont. Maria says it's the busiest the pub's been for years.

Maria, Mitchell, Gabe and I are behind the bar serving the food and drinks – hot chocolate, mulled cider, beer, milky coffee. Maria is beaming. She has assumed the state of grace she usually attains when things get really busy. She moves around quickly, smoothly, somehow doing every-thing at once, as if she has six arms. I, on the other hand, am getting flustered. Still, they'll be lighting the fire soon, and judging the pumpkin-carving competition, and that'll give us a bit of a break. And we're not going to serve the toffee and the toffee-apples; we'll just put them out for people to help themselves, so the night will get easier.

'I think it's really working, Maria,' I say, when we get a moment together by the hotdogs. 'Everybody seems happy. This was a really good idea.'

She just grins.

In what feels like no time at all, she's ringing the last-orders bell and shouting, 'Everybody outside! Bring the pumpkins! Everybody outside!'

The pub starts to empty and once everybody's gone, we go too – then I realise that Maria's not coming down to the fire with me but is hanging back near the entrance. I turn and raise an eyebrow.

'Just in case of thieving bastards,' she says. 'You go and have a good time.'

'But your pumpkin—!' I start.

'If I win, shout me and we'll swap. It's just over the road, Edie, I can see it from here.'

The carved pumpkins are laid out along the embank-ment that separates the road from the beach. They all have candles inside them which gutter pleasingly in the slight breeze. It's a perfect night for an event like this: chilly enough, but not bitter, and it's not raining.

There are traditional jack o' lantern type efforts, hollowed out with two round eyes, a triangular nose and a zig-zaggy slit for a mouth. Some of them look like they've been made by children, with stray knife strokes everywhere and unevenly sized features: badly hacked-up vegetables that are clumsily made but endearing. In fact, there are a lot of children around tonight. The Tup isn't the kind of pub you often see children in, but they're out in force now, wrapped up in scarves and gloves and wellies, all hovering around the pumpkins, holding sparklers and hotdogs. Their laughter is clearer than any other sound.

Then there are the more ornate variations, very detailed and carefully shaped faces with horns or hair or beards or individual teeth. One family has used turnips and turned them into genuinely scary, wizened little goblin heads.

The hot vegetable smell of them is wonderful, and the way they all face out towards the sea, like they're waiting, tugs at something inside me. Their eyes are alive with the light inside. The children crowd around them as if they can communicate with each little flame. Mrs Cook walks slowly up and down the embankment, studying the carvings.

Flames flicker in the heart of the man-made mountain on the sand, and a cheer goes up. Men raise plastic glasses full of beer into the air. Gabe and his friends – I can see Billy, David and Ed – are whooping and charging through the crowd carrying a Guy Fawkes that they've made. He's got a small brown paper bag for a head with a cartoon face drawn onto it. People laugh as the Guy is passed up to Jason, who has clambered back onto the bonfire to receive it. He places the Guy in an armchair that tops the structure.

I want to shout, 'Jason, get off the fire!' but he knows what he's doing; he's already jumped down, and is making his get-away.

The flames grow slowly and people accumulate, pressing up against the fence – although it's not really a fence, more a safe-distance marker: some tape tied to metal poles stuck in the sand.

I wonder if we should have arranged some music, a band, or a sound-system, but as time goes on it becomes obvious that entertainment beyond the fire would have been unnecessary. People want the fire, they want the heat and the comfort and the company – that's what they came for: for the ritual, for each other.

I stand and watch. I feel like I'm observing from the sidelines, but I'm not, I'm somewhere in the middle.

The flames have reached the Guy now and they lick up around his tatty old throne, around his once-smart shoes and his newspaper legs. His trousers catch, then his body, and then his head lolls back. Apart from the fire, he suddenly looks like Granddad used to look when he fell asleep in front of the TV, his arms dangling down the sides of the armchair, his legs out in front, his head tipped back so that his throat looked long and stretched.

There's a clanging sound. It's Mrs Cook, holding two small saucepans above her head and smacking them together. 'Quiet please!' she's shouting. 'The winner of the pumpkin competition is about to be announced! Everybody! Quiet please!' Eventually the message percolates through and she can put the pans down.

'Okay,' she says, 'thank you so much for all of your entries. The standard was of course very high, but there can only be one winner in the end. I've spent some time deliberating, but to be honest I feel like the winning pumpkin chose me in the end – he's irresistible! And, in case you hadn't already guessed, it's this charming fellow right here.' She steps aside to reveal a large Devil pumpkin – and it's only right that it won, really: it must have taken its creator days. An apparently random pattern of swirls and whorls and contours covers it, and yet somehow manifests on one side as an incredibly detailed, grinning Mephistopheles. The prize is a three-course meal for two with wine at The Tup, which is obviously a damned good prize. Mrs Cook leans over it to read the carver's name.

'And so, the winner is – Taylor! Taylor? No, that's it. Just the one name. Is Taylor here?'

As a round of applause gets underway, the young contractor who likes his bacon soft steps through the crowd. He's grinning widely. He's still wearing his black suit and white shirt. He leans in to give Mrs Cook a hug.

I feel drunk, but I don't know if I've had anything to drink.

The first firework goes up, so Jason must be over on the other side of the estuary now. I feel like I can see him, crouching down with a taper and a torch. He's got a big stripy jumper on tonight so his tattoos aren't visible. I imagine that he's grinning like a big kid. The firework is a rocket; it explodes into green rain, the shower of sparks distorting my sense of perspective, and it's followed by another, then two more, then five more, all the same. He must have set them up in a row. He should be using a timer or something, but he's probably just lighting them one by one, judging by the disregard for his own safety that he demonstrated on the bonfire.

Oh, Jason. I suddenly ache for him; not in a romantic or sexual way, but . . . I don't know. It's affection. I want to give him a hug. I want to say, *Thank you Jason, thank you for coming here and being kind to people.*

The fireworks are a delight. They shatter in the sky and are reflected in the thin layer of water that remains in the centre of the estuary so that it looks like there are explosions going on below the surface of the world. People are making the *Ooooh!* sounds that they are supposed to make, laughing and pointing up and down and cheering. Everywhere I look there are scarves and woolly hats and waterproof jackets. When people are looking up at the sky and smiling, their faces are younger and firmer and prettier.

The bonfire is reflected too, and the effect is magnificent. It looks almost spherical; a fiery orb surrounded by people, floating in a sea of multicoloured sparks.

I go back to the bar.

The clean-up is scheduled for tomorrow morning, but judging by the bulging bin-bags out the front of The Tup, people have been pretty good at discarding their paper plates and plastic pint glasses properly, so hopefully it won't be too big a job. I finish my cigarette and watch the guests disperse from the smouldering remains of the fire; some are going home straight away; others are coming in for a drink. I wait until there's nobody else around and then head back inside as well.

'I might go to bed,' I tell Maria, 'if you don't need me any more.'

'You do that, Edie,' she says. She is the happiest I've seen her for a long time. She nods at Gabe, who's behind the bar again. 'I've got my boy helping,' she says. 'He is a good boy.'

'You're drunk,' I say, and lean over the bar to give her a hug. 'Here. Have you seen Jason around? Has he been back since the fireworks?'

'I don't know,' Maria says. 'He must be here somewhere – maybe in the gents? Do you want me to give him a message?'

'No, don't worry about it. I'll see him tomorrow or something. Just wanted to say thank you for doing such a good job tonight.'

'You and me both,' Maria says. She smiles. 'Goodnight, Edie.'

'Goodnight,' I say.

*　　　*　　　*

I see John Senior sitting in his bedroom. It has a double bed. If I didn't know better, I'd say the room was still John and Christina's; it has been kept impeccably. The bedding is neat and clean, and there are cushions and throws scattered tastefully around. The walls are a peachy colour and one standard lamp casts a warm glow. There is a photo on one of the bedside tables – just of Christina, her long dark hair falling across her face, a bright smile visible. John's slippers are placed carefully beside the bed. The carpet is thick and looks soft. John himself is curled up on his side on the bed, one arm outstretched towards the window, which I can see has boards nailed across the outside of it. Something is banging on the window, hard, and there is light shining in through the cracks between the boards, and John is waving his hand at the window, as if to say 'No, no, don't come in, please', and he's crying, too.

Chapter Eighteen

I see Phillip drunkenly patting at his pockets after returning home. I see him patting his coat pockets and then his trouser pockets and then rooting around inside all of them, one after the other, and then he goes through them again. He tips his head back and closes his eyes and grunts. He stumbles away from the front door and round the side of his semi-detached house, and then bends over at the back door, both hands creeping along until they find the edge of one of those bristly brown 'Welcome' mats. He goes down on one knee, lifts the mat up and claws at something underneath: a key for the back door. He eventually manages to get it into the lock, twists it and more or less falls through the door. As he gets inside I hear him laughing to himself, the kind of laughter that suggests personal satisfaction, as if maybe he feels that he has achieved something.

I see him turn back around, bend down, and put the key under the mat.

It is one a.m. and I am in the caravan and I am still completely awake. But tonight I am awake intentionally, fully-dressed and everything. In my hands I hold Phillip's back-door key, successfully liberated from beneath the doormat in the early hours of yesterday morning. And now is the time to use it.

There's a faint howling sound on the air tonight. I stand for a moment on the main road, trying to discern which direction it's coming from, but I can't. It's a clear night, the first in a while, and I can smell smoke. The stars are out. The Milky Way itself is visible, a fuzzy-edged blue band arcing from one horizon to the other. I stare at it for a short while until I get vertiginous and start to feel that I am upside down. The howling is similar to a human voice, except it's an inarticulate pain-filled ululation that just continues, as if lung capacity is not an issue. It is very faint indeed, so much so that I start to wonder if it is really there at all.

As I get closer to Phillip's house, I become aware that there are not many lights on. Ravenglass, as a rule, does not have many lights on at one or two o'clock in the morning, but tonight the village is even darker than usual.

I let myself quietly in through the back door, suddenly very excited. I feel as if this is almost the reason for my gift, for my visions: to identify Phillip as the killer and rapist that he surely is, to find the proof.

His kitchen is a disgrace: unwashed dishes everywhere, and greasy water with oil floating on it in the sink. No washing-up bowl. Food packaging strewn all over the place.

I've seen his living room before, of course. I creep through it and then up the stairs. The stairs are creaky and feel weak, as if they're made from very thin wood. From here – halfway up – I can hear Phillip snoring. He keeps on snoring, despite the creaking stairs.

I get to the landing. His bedroom door is open. I can see him bundled up in bed, a big bulge beneath white covers, bathed in the blue light of the stars and the Milky Way outside. He's left his curtains open, which seems strange to me, given his personal predilections, but then, I can't claim to know him deeply, even after having watched him engaging in some of his most intimate behaviours. What does it take to know a person? I have seen Phillip do a lot of things that he would not want anybody else to see, but even so, I don't know him – though why equate watching somebody to knowing them? That is another question. I suppose there is a part of me that thinks people reveal themselves when they are on their own, and maybe they do, but to know somebody – in the way that two married people know each other, I mean, which is about as closely as any one person on this planet can know another person, probably – requires more than that.

Conversation is one thing – a major thing. Seeing somebody when they are ill and looking after them, that might be another. I knew my grandparents pretty well. When somebody lets you down in a major way I suppose you learn a lot about them then, in that instance of being let down, that hot, burning kind of disappointment that you feel and you try to deny, but you've felt it, you know you have, and nothing you can do will ever change that. And then another question, a third question is: how much do you really want to know another person, when it comes down to it? Do you want to know what they think when they're on their own, looking in the mirror? And even if you do want to know a person, even if that knowing itself is unquestionably a good thing – which I don't think it is, personally – is it worth the price you have to pay? Is it worth being let down? Is it worth the accumulation of tiny rituals, tiny comforts, that in the end cause untold grief? Looking at somebody looking at themselves in the mirror, when they think they're on their own, completely: is it worth that? I don't know.

But anyway, his curtains are open, which surprises me. Given his activities, given the vaguely paranoid tone that accompanies a lot of his bigotry, given the hysterical fear that drives his blog posts, I would have expected him to close his curtains before bed. However . . .

He is snoring like a big drunken pig. He's lying on his back with his mouth wide open, his red chin – red from being badly shaven – pressed into his chest because of all the pillows under his head. Even in this dim light I can see that the pillows are discoloured, yellowed with dirt. He looks fatter like this. His eyes are closed and his eyelids, which obviously I never see that much of, are very blue and veiny. I turn to his wardrobe. It's a plain one, and the door opens easily and silently. I reach up to the shoeboxes where he keeps his older photos, the especially incriminating ones. I find the one that I watched him put the wallets back into. I take it down and hold it to my chest with one hand and then close the wardrobe.

Phillip stops snoring very suddenly, halfway through a snore, resulting in a very immediate and total silence. I freeze for a second or two and then slowly turn around and he is sitting up in bed looking at me. His mouth is still wide open and his eyes are fixed on the shoebox. The expression on his face is a very pathetic, total fear; a kind of horror, really. I hadn't wanted to wake him up because I thought that maybe he would attack me – I'm an invader, an intruder, trespassing on his personal property, his land, this patch of earth he's laid claim to, stuck his flag into – *bought*, I guess; he's put money down for it, which is as close as we get these days to bloody hunting and gathering. Unless we actually go out and bloodily hunt and gather, that is. So all that work he's done, for all that money, for this house, and here I am, making a mockery of it, of the point of all that ownership. I thought he'd be angry – I thought he'd be inspired to towering, incandescent fury, totally confident in his rightness, in his rage.

But no.

He climbs out of bed. He's wearing too-small boxers and a baggy T-shirt. I dart towards the door, but he's in front of me, blocking the way. He puts his hands on my shoulders. A cold clamminess creeps up my neck.

'Drop the box,' he says, quietly. His breath is intensely bad: stale alcohol and tooth-rot. I shake my head and try to get away, but he's actually quite strong and he digs his fingertips into me and his nails are long enough to hurt. He pushes me back against the wall beside the wardrobe, lets go of me and grabs the box. I let go of the box and put my hands around his throat, forcing my thumbs into the soft bit below his Adam's apple. He chokes and flails around and drops the box, then grabs for my wrists.

I can feel blood welling up around my thumbs. I let go of him and when he staggers backwards I bend down and pick up the box and run out of the room. I can hear him behind me, but I'm halfway down the stairs when something hits me in the back of the head and I fall forwards. I'm falling in empty space for a moment and then sliding head-first down the last few steps, my arms clutched close beneath me, but I don't have the pictures any more. He's coming down the stairs behind me, as clumsily and noisily as a cow might, and I'm waiting for his weight to hit me, but I scramble forwards through the spilled photo wallets now lying all over the floor, and his feet come down just after I've moved out the way, and I'm getting to my feet and dashing through the living room into the kitchen, where I know I left the back door open.

Phillip's hands are at my back, catching my jacket, and he's making the most unpleasant gurgling sounds. He punches me in the back of the head and I feel it all down my back and fall to my knees. I pull myself up using the worktop and in front of me is a kitchen knife that is covered in something dried and crusty. I grab the knife and hold it out and spin around and it cuts him across the face, right across, just above his upper lip. I feel it bump along the surface of his upper front teeth and then his top lip is hanging off, actually hanging off. His mouth is open and then above it is a big slit, so it looks like he's got two mouths, one big one and one small one. Quickly I lunge forwards and stick the knife into his chest where I imagine his heart to be, but it sticks on a rib so I pull it out and jab again and it goes in further this time. He keels over, still gurgling, one hand on his bloody throat and one on his bloody chest, and he thrashes around on the floor. The blood looks black on the pale lino, and as he thrashes around it all gets smeared across the grey, and collects little bits of dirt and mud, because obviously he never bothers to clean it, his kitchen floor, which strikes me as very sad.

I don't leave the kitchen until Phillip has stopped moving, by which point the sky is getting lighter. I walk back through the house, carefully avoiding the blood, which he's trailed all the way down from the bedroom. I must have done more damage than I thought. I gather up the photo wallets, put them in the box, and then come back to the kitchen, where I look at his body for a bit longer. He's definitely not moving. I put my ear to his mangled-up mouth and there's no breath. I can't quite bring myself to check for a pulse, so that'll do.

I close the door behind me and lock it, and then put the key back under the 'Welcome' mat. I wonder if anyone, other than Phillip, has ever crossed the mat. Keith, maybe, though I can't actually imagine that. Keith's relationship with Phillip was more mercenary than friendship. No, Phillip was a very lonely man.

Feeling sorry for people you hate is a sad, complicated thing. I'm very glad that the Candle and the stones have started to simplify my world somewhat, in their own way.

When I get back onto the main road I see that further down towards the beach there are a couple of long dark objects lying on the tarmac. I'm not sure if they're human bodies or other things.

The village is very quiet and still now.

Part Four

. . . would find it hard to believe that I have not yet told you more about the mountains! The truth is, I suppose, that if you live near them you take them for granted, which is a shame, because they are magnificent — cold and unforgiving, and they have taken lives, but magnificent.

One of my favourite mountains is back in Wasdale, and it's called Yewbarrow. Don't they have such funny names? I'm sure the origin of their names must make for some very interesting reading. It's something I can get my teeth into when I come home.

I like Yewbarrow because all the hard work is at the beginning, or at least, that's how it has always seemed to me. It's one short, steep slog, and then you're at the top. Or, I should say, one end of the top, because

Yewbarrow has a long spine, and the majority of the hike is spent walking along that spine. It's a narrow, rocky road up there, which means you feel higher up and more adventurous than you really are. Naturally, the views are just beautiful. You can see right out across all the farms to the sea, if you look to the west, and if you look east there are more mountains — taller mountains, more jagged peaks — and mysterious valleys. Depending on the time of year there might be snow, vast swathes of untouched white snow. Such a magical place. I would that you can come with me on one such hike, one day not too long from now . . .

CHAPTER NINETEEN

Though my grandparents did deteriorate physically – I mean, I had to support them when they wanted to go out for a walk, and for a few years they were not dexterous enough to cook, for example – their minds remained sharp right up until they died. I'm very grateful for this.

The thing that I don't ever want to happen to me is the inevitable ritualisation of certain things, and then what happens when those rituals are no longer possible. My grandparents, every night in bed, would lie facing each other, and Granddad would hug Grandma and say 'Goodnight, petal' and my grandma would say 'Goodnight, bear', and he'd kiss her on her right cheek, and then that meant they could go to sleep, that was the end of the day, right there. Every night. I heard this every night for years and years because there was no distance between my room and theirs – both rooms opened onto the landing, which was just a square at the top of the stairs, and they left their bedroom door open, 'just in case'. Though, just in case of what I never knew. Then, when it got to the point where I was helping them into bed, I would see this ritual enacted. And then, of course, Granddad died, and every night after that my grandma would lie in bed on her left side and not know what to do, and she had real trouble sleeping. I used to hear her say 'Goodnight, bear', but I knew that it was not a comforting thing; it was habit, and it was her at her most lonely, her most alone. It was the direct result of the love they had for each other, and the direct result of a ritual that for decades had provided the most sincere and direct companionship, a ritual that had provided the safest and warmest and happiest of moments, every single night.

And me lying in my bed, listening to her lying in her bed, listening to those words, 'Goodnight, bear', night after night, every night, for three years, listening to that small lonely voice, that was one of my most formative experiences.

CHAPTER TWENTY

—

One morning I'm feeding the contractors – that's what it's like, really, it's like they're pigs waiting at the gate for their swill – and the mood in the room is different. They're sitting at their tables reading their papers or flicking through their phones or whatever, and something is very different. I wonder if it's a greyer day than normal outside, or if I've left some curtains closed somewhere, but I check those things and no, it's nothing like that. All of the skin in the room is pallid. All of the eyes are angry.

It's nearing the end of the breakfast period when I take a plate out – fried mushrooms, fried bread, nothing else – to a contractor whose nickname is Whistler. He never whistles as far as I know. Anyway, I'm putting the plate on his table and he looks down at it – he is a big man, with bad acne scars and a gold stud in one ear, and thick glasses –

and he opens his mouth and his tongue just kind of falls out – not that it's become detached, but it's grown very long and flabby – and he jumps back shouting and his tongue trails after him, pulling a load of mushrooms off the plate as it goes. He grabs it and holds it up to his eyes and stares at it and it's very *white*, really, for a tongue; it's very pale indeed. He looks at me and I just look back, but it's hard to maintain eye-contact, because my eyes keep flicking to his tongue, unintentionally. He moans a bit and then runs out of the room and clomps up the stairs.

You would expect most people – though not me, perhaps – to react strongly to such a scene, but the other contractors just get on with their eating. I stand there for a moment longer wondering if there's going to be some kind of delayed shock, but eventually a couple of them just look up at me, vaguely annoyed, as if to say, *What are you still doing here?*

I turn to go, and in doing so I notice that one of the men has stuck his fork into the back of his right hand, which is palm-down on the table. He's looking at it kind of vacantly, as if he's waiting for it to do something. I feel like I should go over to him, but my feet are just carrying me on through the door into the kitchen, where I try to get on with some work, but I can't. I'm shaking like a shitting dog, as John Senior might say when he's feeling coarse. I lean back into a corner and put my hands out to the stainless steel worktops on either side.

CHAPTER TWENTY-ONE

It is as I am returning one morning from a night-time drive that I see what looks like a tall man with no skin scampering up from the estuary sands and over the grassy ridge. It runs on all fours into the main road in front of my car and stops and looks at me through the early-morning gloom. Its eyes are opaque, and like two big yellow pennies, a jaundiced milky bony colour. It is not quite a de-skinned human being; its limbs are not quite right for it to be that, but it is very bloody. I stop the car. It looks away and continues over the road and I watch as it makes its way along the fronts of the little houses, smashes the glass of a front window and disappears inside.

Fear is not quite what it engendered within me, for some reason; it was more a fascination, recognition, an *I knew this was coming* – although I hadn't foreseen such a thing. What I mean is, now I've seen it, it feels like it was inevitable all along; a consequence of the collapsing of the Elsewhere into our own world.

It's not until I'm parking the car that I wonder, was it the Candle? But no, it was not the Candle; I would have felt the Candle before I saw it, and somehow I would have communicated with it, or, rather, it would have somehow communicated with me. This was some other kind of beast, and where there's one, there might be more. I will have to be careful. The Candle's promise not to harm me – I believe it, but whether or not the Candle controls the thing I've just seen I don't know.

I'm locking the car when I hear screams. There are no other sounds this morning, just screams; they get hoarser and more distant, as if the person screaming is being taken away, somewhere to the north of here. Then once the screaming has stopped, which it does suddenly, the sea-gulls start up, squealing and squawking as if what happened has happened to one of their own, as if they understand.

Chapter Twenty-Two

It's after work and I'm in the bar, drinking, thinking that I could do with some sleep tonight and getting drunk might be a good way to precipitate that. Phillip is not here, of course, and neither are either of the Johns Platt. Gabe is, though, and Maria, naturally.

As Maria rings the last orders bell the door bursts open and a man with a floor-length black coat and teeth protruding from all over his face bounds in. I drop my pint and fall off my stool and crawl, shivering, around to the end of the bar and then behind it. I look over the top of it, peering between the beer pumps.

The man has no eyes or nose or anything; he has only half a head, with the front half sheared off, but he's got a lot more teeth than most people, and they're not all in one place; they're jutting out at all angles from the mess that's in the place you'd expect his face to be. He stalks down the bar and there are even teeth – human teeth, I mean – sticking out of the back of his head, which is quite soft-looking, for a head.

Why is nobody screaming? I duck back down and vomit, copiously.

Maria looks down at me. 'Second time tonight he's been in,' she says. 'He came in while you were in the kitchen. Must be hungry.'

Then there is a scream, a brief one, followed by a growl and a sucking sound, and I look back over the bar and the man-thing is bent over Keith, of all people, rubbing its teeth into his neck and feeding on the blood that's coming out. The bar is silent, apart from the sucking and glugging. After a few minutes of this the creature pulls Keith from his barstool and drags him along the floor and out of the door, through which I catch a glimpse of the rain, which has come back.

I stand up and Gabe looks at me, his eyes wide. 'That guy freaks me out a little bit, man,' he says. 'All those teeth!'

'Yeah,' I say. I should say something else, but can't. My heartbeat and breathing are all wrong, and if I try to think about speaking, one or the other might stop.

'Edie,' Maria says, 'why the sick?'

'That monster,' I say. 'Aren't you alarmed, or disgusted?'

Maria throws both her hands up. 'It's just the world we live in, Edie! I wish it weren't!'

I nod. It is the world we live in, now, I suppose. I would

have expected everyone else, everyone to whom these things should be surprising, to react more strongly, but maybe part of the world changing is that everybody changes with it so they don't see how much it does change, they don't see how fucked up it actually is. The field that is expanding from Greycroft is reshaping people's minds as it simultaneously reshapes the world.

I clean up my sick, which I'm very embarrassed about now, and then I use the same mop and bucket to go and clean up the blood from the stone bar floor. People have been very careful not to tread in the blood. I get a couple of sympathetic nods from the contractors and the reporters. The reporters are all very quiet these days, and didn't even get their cameras out when that toothy man-thing came in. They just eat and drink and talk in low voices to each other.

After mopping, I get a sponge and try to wipe down the padded seat of the stool that Keith had been sitting on, but it's soaked in pretty bad.

Chapter Twenty-Three

I don't know what day it is. I'm standing in the kitchen with the oven on, ready to do breakfasts. I've got a meat cleaver in my hand. I wait for an hour, an hour and a half, before I hear movement upstairs – creaking floorboards and slow, heavy footsteps – and I hear somebody descend. I wouldn't have waited so long but I can't think coherently enough to do much else.

I wait until I hear whoever it is sit down in the dining room, and then slowly walk to the door and try to peer around the frame without being seen.

It's Pitbull. He's sitting at one of the far tables with his back to me. His tattooed arms are just hanging by his sides, and his shoulders are slumped. From here, his ears look a bit big, and . . . dark.

I put the meat cleaver in my apron pocket and walk out into the room. 'Hey, Pitbull,' I say, but my voice betrays my nervousness and breaks.

He straightens his back a little bit, and lifts his head up, but doesn't reply.

'Where have you been?' I ask.

He still doesn't speak.

'Pitbull,' I say.

Nothing.

I don't want to get any closer.

'Hey!' I shout. I throw my notepad at him and it hits him square in between the shoulderblades.

He jerks forward when it hits him and then stands up and slowly turns around to face me. He supports himself using the chair. His eyes are hanging out and he's had a massive nosebleed. His nostrils are distorted and his nose is all squashed out of shape. His ears are torn up and misshapen.

He taps his temple. 'Been trying to get at it,' he says, his voice wavering. 'I'm sick of my brain and I've been trying to get at it.'

His hands are caked in blood.

'Maybe you can get at it,' he says.

I shake my head.

He comes towards me, holding his hands out in front of him, clearly not able to see. I wonder if his eyes are still relaying messages – showing him his feet and the floor as he stumbles along. I back into a table and knock it over, trip over it, and land on my backside, hitting my coccyx. I take the meat cleaver out of my apron.

Pitbull takes each eyeball between the thumb and fore-finger of each hand and tries to angle them forwards, so he can see. Eventually he has them angled at me.

'I can't see very well,' he says. 'What's that you've got there?'

'A cleaver,' I whisper.

'Can't hear very well either. Are you talking?'

'It's a meat cleaver,' I say, more loudly.

'Will you open my head up and get this thing out?' he asks.

'No,' I say.

'Then give me that.'

'No.'

He moves towards me again but he trips and falls too, and he lands on top of me, squashing my ribcage and pinning me to the ground. He finds the cleaver, grabs it with both hands and then rolls off.

I shuffle away and try to regain my breath. Pitbull remains there on his back and as I look at him, he brings the meat cleaver down hard into his forehead.

'No!' I shout, but my voice is drowned out by his screams. He wasn't holding the cleaver straight, so although the blade pierced the skin it just followed the curve of his skull round to the side of his head, carving a large swathe away from the bone. Blood sprays out. But he's trying again.

I jump up and, as he lifts the cleaver up above him for a second time I try to grab it. But it's slippery now, and he kicks at my shins.

'Let me do this, Edie!' he says, the words bubbling out through fresh blood. 'I don't want to be in this Hell any more.'

He plants a foot into my stomach and I flail backwards, hands slipping from the cleaver.

This time his blow is more accurate and more powerful; he buries the blade deep. His body jerks and twitches, involuntarily moving across the floor like a vibrating mobile phone.

No. Not Pitbull.

I run from the room, but realise that I've forgotten something. I turn back at the door and look at Pitbull. I know what I need to do, but I don't know if I can. I return to Pitbull's body and kneel down. I put a hand on his chest – his heart is thudding out like a full-term baby's kicks – and, with the other, try to yank the cleaver from his forehead. Yet more blood splashes out, but the blade does not come free. 'I'm sorry,' I say. 'I'm sorry.' I set my jaw and try again. I feel like I can hear the metal squeaking against the bone.

The strength required to bury this so deeply is enormous. It must have been strength born of desperation.

I close my eyes as I feel the blade loosen, and then – with an awful sucking sound - it finally comes free.

I head out of the front door, lighting a cigarette as I go. It's a cold, dry day. There's a car, stationary, in the middle of the road. Two other cars have stopped behind it. They're all empty. The windows of the first one are broken and the driver's door is open and there's blood all over it.

I head round to my own car and sit for a moment. That moaning on the wind can be heard here, now, along with the hissing and clicking that, previously, I could only hear at Greycroft.

I close my eyes and see the stones, now thin, sharp and sizeless. They're visible to me like the Candle is visible, existing in a different way to the mere physical objects that they once were, or that I thought they were. They make their own sound: a thrumming, pylon sound, like electrical wires. I feel like the stones extend infinitely upwards into space, and also infinitely downwards into space at the other end, like a long, narrow cylinder that threads through the Earth. I feel as if that is their true shape, not the worn, weathered knobs of rock that everybody sees when they look at them.

This has to end now.

I turn the key in the ignition and set off.

I park at Newton Manor as usual, turn off the engine

and get out of the car. The grass remains frosted in the shadows of the house. The house looks at me, but I don't look back at it. I run down the lane towards the field where the stone circle is, and get there a lot more quickly than I was expecting to, more quickly than I should have. It has grown, spilled out of its original field.

The area of new, strange grass has expanded outwards in all directions. The hedgerows that were there are still here, but they look different now, woodier, thicker and taller and more dense, and the fences are ancient-looking, all slack and sagging.

It has expanded so far that the field is nearly at Newton Manor, and nearly at Sellafield on the other side. It's lapping at the boundaries. What will happen when it expands into Sellafield? I don't know – though, of course, if Ravenglass is anything to go by, the effects will already be making themselves known. This dark grass is only a physical symptom of something larger, something more pronounced and more widespread than this particular symptom indicates.

I imagine the powers that be at Sellafield are keeping it quiet so as to delay the inevitable PR problems that'll hit them when all of this becomes news. People will point the finger at Sellafield at first, albeit only for a short while.

That's if the management have even noticed anything

wrong. The effects might yet be scattered and subtle. And, as in Ravenglass, their witnesses may not realise what they're seeing.

I take a deep breath and then step onto the new grass. The hissing and clicking is immediately louder, and yes, I can hear other things now, snorting and buzzing and other sounds for which I don't have the words. There is a cloud of big flies hanging over the field and they're hovering, waiting.

I can see the stones, and they're even sharper and blacker and taller than they were last time I saw them. They're growing. A seeping mist hides the ground around them and I think I can see small things moving within it. I take a few more steps in that direction, my right hand on the handle of the cleaver, but then I see that the soil beneath the new grass is full of big black worms, and they're crawling up onto my shoes, and I can't bear it, I really can't, and I'm running away in the opposite direction, back towards the house.

That's when I hear a scream and it's a voice I know. The scream is coming from Newton Manor, and then there are other voices, all screaming, all coming from the same place, and then like a bomb going off in my head the Candle's light is blaring out behind my eyes and it's here, now, close to me, and the screams get louder and the light gets brighter and I stumble and fall forwards and put my hands out and

I feel the earth writhing beneath them, things moving between my fingers. I see thick worms flop upwards and across the backs of my hands, leaving sticky trails, and I convulse, violently. My head is on fire with light, the bright white light of the sun, and it's there in my head whether my eyes are open or closed.

I stand back up and shake my hands and keep on going. The light is fading now, receding to its normal level.

As I finally escape the new grass, it hits me: the Candle had hidden itself from me and then accidentally revealed itself. I say accidentally because I felt it lose control, I felt it get excited, I felt a coruscating white heat of excitement, a total lapse, an unintentional flare-up. I felt the mask slipping.

The voice I recognised, that was Maria. I can still hear her, screaming and shouting, from somewhere within the house that stands before me. The air gets colder as I move towards Newton Manor. The grass crunches beneath my feet. Winter is here. There are big black birds croaking in the trees, but I can hear that screaming too, and laughing, grunting, clicking . . . and, as I get closer, I can hear something being thrown around, smashing into walls. I can hear stamping and punching, and doors slamming.

The door opens when I push it. Inside, immediately inside, there is blood on the floor, not just drops of it or smears, but blood wall-to-wall, deep enough to splash in. I push the door open wider. The screams are coming from upstairs, but as I step through the doorway, they stop, and all of the other noises stop too. I can smell damp and shit, and something like turkey giblets: a rotten, offally smell.

There are naked bodies of men and women strewn across the hallway, dismembered, ripped up, half-eaten. All kinds of bodily fluids are splattered over the faded wallpaper. It's colder in here than it was outside.

I hear movement in a room to the right and I take out the meat cleaver and hold it firmly. I peer in through the doorway. This room has dark green wallpaper with a pattern of large fleshily-red flowers on it, peeling from the walls. A rectangle of light is bright on the floor, and the rotting, stained floorboards within it are starkly lit. There's a cupboard in an alcove in one dark corner of the room and it's open. Inside it there's an ancient, yellowed dustpan and brush. There's another dead body pressed against the wall beneath the window. I can't see what might have made the noise. Then there's a rustle and a wheeze and something drops from the ceiling and lands on its feet like a cat, but it's dog-sized. It has a human head and it bares its teeth at me, but it hobbles backwards as if it's scared and I realise that it's got spiny bones protruding from the end of its limbs rather than proper, actual feet. Its skin is pale pink and vaguely loose. It is a horrible thing. I walk slowly backwards, until I'm out of the room, and then I press my back against the wall.

I've done this. *Me.*

There's another creature staring at me from another doorway. This is the big yellow-eyed thing I saw in the road. It's drooling and panting and picking away inside an exposed ribcage with one of its hands. There's also something crouched in the darkness of the stairs that descend down to the cellar and the wet-room.

This might be it, now. This might be where they get it together and kill me.

There's a noise from upstairs: a long, loud creak, the weight of something shifting. The creak is followed by scraping, and then a thump, then another thump.

They won't hurt you, Edie.

As the Candle's voices swirl around, the creatures cower and dribble and retreat into the shadowy recesses.

Come upstairs.

'What are you doing?' I shout.

Come upstairs. You can do this. You are not like normal people. You do not just run screaming. You understand the weaknesses of normal people and have defeated them. Come upstairs.

I do as it says. There's more blood, of course. The carpeted stairs are sodden; my feet make a wet sound with every step. I hear things moving behind me; I look back down into the hallway. It's now full of things, some of them more humanoid than others, all of them different sizes, some of them skinless, and some pale and shiny, some on all fours and some bipedal, some with hands and some with sharpened bones, some gendered and some not. They're creeping up from the cellar, out of the doorways that open onto the hall and, in the case of the smallest ones, from out of the bodies that are lying, dead, in the muck.

There's a faint whisper from the bare trees outside and the open front door creaks ever so gently as it moves slightly in the breeze. But the birds have gone quiet. Newton Manor is silently waiting. I look up to the landing. This storey is darker than the ground floor.

There's a scraping sound again.

One point of light up there is a gleaming brass doorknob, and I feel grateful for it as my eyes fix on that bright spot. I remember the film *Bedknobs and Broomsticks*; I remember watching it at my grandparents' house, lying on the floor and looking up at the TV in a way that makes my neck hurt just thinking about it.

The film is playing out in front of my eyes. I can hear the songs, *really* hear them. Grandma puts a plate of biscuits down just in front of me and I reach out for one and my hand passes in front of my eyes and I see again where I am, here at Newton Manor, of course. I shake my head, but the confusion is not in front of my eyes, it's behind them, and shaking my head makes no difference to anything. And anyway, this is a doorknob, not a bedknob.

I continue up the stairs, still staring at the doorknob. I

know that this is where the Candle is. Will I be able to see it, finally? I reach out to open the door and something drips onto my hand and I look up and even in the darkness I can see that more dead bodies have been arranged around the doorway. They have been nailed to the frame.

I open the door.

The Candle is seated in a big green armchair at the end of the room. The chair is worn and canted forwards. It's missing a foot. The room stinks of decomposing flesh; various bodies are arranged in poses all around it. The man with teeth for a face stands behind the chair; no doubt the bodies are his harvest.

The Candle is wearing a hooded black cloak from which two bony hands protrude. I can't see its face but some kind of fluid is hanging down from the darkness of the hood – drool or blood or phlegm or something. I can't make out what colour it is against the black fabric.

The hands are long-fingered and grey-skinned, patterned with pale blue – old, faded tattoos. The tattoos are geometric. On the back of each hand is a concentric circle design, but before I can make out any more the hands start fidgeting and the fingers start jerking like the legs of dying insects.

Are you bringing your blood to me now?

'No,' I say. I'm looking at a body lying at the Candle's feet. Maria. She is covered in filth and her blonde hair is red. The tooth man is hissing, I think, though I can't really tell where the sound is coming from.

I put my left hand to my mouth and crouch down. I hold the flat of the cleaver against the side of my head. 'I didn't want this,' I say.

You wanted Phillip Banks. That was what you got. The changes that have come, that are coming – you had no knowledge of them. You are not to blame.

'I helped you.'

Yes, you did.

'What are you doing? What do you want?'

I have told you. I have been waiting for a chance to come back here again. To come back to this bleak mountainous region; this protuberance on England's side, where I began. I never thought I would get the chance, but the idea of it has been alive in me for these thousands of years, a fire that has never stopped burning: the chance to come home, to be corporeal again – to rule as I once ruled. I am a ruler. I have ruled in my time away. I have become Chieftain, Lord, King, Tsar, Emperor, God-King, over different peoples. I have risen to sit upon throne after throne, in halls of gold, of ice, of fire, of bone. I have ridden in the vanguard of armies willing to die at my word. I have travelled and I have conquered and I have eaten the flesh of my enemies and I have turned their skeletons into toys for my Elsewhere spawn. I have painted my palaces and my face with their fresh hot blood. In the Elsewhere, I have carved out my domain. But not here. Not here. Not yet.

Imagine: through night I am riding a dead horse over an expanse of cinder. The horse is a part of me. The cinders are black and sharp. The sky above is riven and red; brown clouds boil at the horizon.

Our hooves crush the cinders into dust. Amongst the dust are bones and small metal trinkets. There is a shrieking on the air. I am approaching a stone circle; the menhirs are tall and rounded and look like the tips of giant fingers protruding from the ground. The horse is bleeding from its eyes. My forearms are buried in the back of the horse. Behind me on the plain is a herd of hundreds of dead horses, their eyes milky-white, their teeth bared, the remains of their manes writhing in the wind as they gallop aimlessly across the wastes.

That is the world I envisage.

'I don't want that. You didn't tell me what you wanted.'

Edie, you wanted the end of the world. You saw it beginning and you let it continue. You didn't care. Now my power is touching people; changing their minds, shaping their thoughts, corrupting their bodies. And maybe you don't like that. But it's too late – at least for some.

'Well,' I say, 'no, I'm not going to help you any more. I'm not going to bleed for you any more. You can kill me. I don't care.'

The Candle's hands snap into tight fists and it sits up in the chair, its back rigid. Its fists shake. The tooth man laughs through his crowded mouth-hole.

Then the Candle relaxes and leans back. *You won't bleed for me? Very well. But withholding your blood won't send me back. I'm here now, for ever.*

'I don't care. I'm not giving you any more. My blood – you need it for something, I don't know what, but you do.'

The tooth man steps forwards, his arms reaching out in front of him, but the Candle stops him with the back of his hand.

Yes. The Candle's voices are icy and distant. *You infuriate me, Edie Grace, but you are correct. Your blood is valuable to me; it has a use. However, I will keep my word: I will not hurt you. I remain ever grateful for the chance you have given me; for the presence you have enabled – for the domain your blood engendered.* He points in the direction of Greycroft, the stone circle. *The domain you've seen, and felt.* He points at the tooth man. *The followers who have come through the stones, and those who have yet to come. I have a kingdom now, Edie, even if only small, and that is your doing, so thank you. Every drop of blood you gave expanded the radius of the circle of my rule a little more. If you gave me more blood, then it would grow yet further, and I would grant you power within it. Alternatively, if you want to leave, you are free to go. But know that I cannot control the things that are now roaming the vicinity; my voice can only be heard so far. To be safe, you will have to leave my domain entirely; these creatures cannot exist outside of it. Get out of the reach of the stones. And do not come back.*

'I'm going to kill you first.'

No. The voices are agonised shrieks. The Candle stands up. It is taller than I realised, and moves quickly. It points to the door behind me. *Get out, Edie. Leave now before my patience deserts me. And don't delude yourself; you cannot hurt me.*

I heft the cleaver and step forwards, but the tooth man again puts his arms out and moves in front of the Candle. I stop moving and so does he. I lower the cleaver and turn and run.

He chases me.

I hit the wall at the bottom of the first flight of stairs and, without thinking, jump through the window, breaking it with my shoulder. The glass shatters in a brittle explosion of sparkling shards. Outside, the day is still bright. For a moment the shards and I hang in the air, and there is no sound, and then I am falling into shadow, into the mossy unlit passage that runs between the house and the walled garden. My shoulder slams into the far wall and I bounce back and my head slams into the wall of the house. I land on the unforgiving paving stones and the left ankle snaps – I hear it, but I don't feel it, not yet. It's the adrenalin, or something. I know I just need to go: I need to get into the sunlight.

I'm hopping, limping, dragging myself along the path. He could jump down and catch me here – I'm still in the dark. The paving stones go on for ever. The walls are getting higher; the passage is getting longer; the corner of the house is getting further away. I slip on the slimy moss that coats the stone and fall on my back. I turn my head and see an infestation of woodlice crawling out of a crack in the wall. I take a deep breath and sit up, but the simplest movements are so hard – I can feel my ankle now and it's burning. I don't look behind me; I just need to keep going. I've dropped the cleaver somewhere. I don't know if the tooth man is chasing me or not, but I can't stop to check.

I make it. I want to collapse when I get out of the shadowy passageway, but I don't. I can't. I carry on around the house until I get to the car.

I get in the car and turn the key in the ignition and go to put the thing into first gear and then realise that I can't use my left foot – it's not just the pain; the foot is limp, out of my control. I try again, just pushing down on the foot as if it's a loose shoe or something. What's happening to me? I try again, and this time I get the pressure and though my ankle is howling at me to stop, I manage to push the pedal down for long enough to get out of neutral and into first. I don't feel like I'm inside my body: I can feel the pain, but it's abstract, detached from me.

I look up at the sky to make sure it's still daytime because everything seems dark, but the sun is still high. *Okay, go.* I set off and turn the car around and escape the clearing in front of the house. I'm driving back down the lonnin. The trees that surround Newton Manor are on my right.

I go for second gear. It's getting easier to ignore the pain. If I think of my foot as something else – something not of my body – attached to the end of my leg then I can do it. Getting away is more important than avoiding pain, anyway.

Third.

I'm going faster now. Good: I need to get away before the tooth man comes. I don't know where I'm going though. I—

I forgot about that bend. I stamp on the brake pedal and—

Oh fuck oh shit oh no. Something twists; bone grinds against bone. My foot slips off the brake and onto the accelerator and the car lurches forwards and ploughs straight into the rocky dyke. There's a crunch and a squeal, a second crunch, a choking, spluttering sound.

I open my eyes. Something is thundering inside my head: a wave breaking, blood pounding, or just pouring. Or—

The sound fades away. It's coming from above: a fighter jet.

I look through the windscreen. The bonnet has crumpled. The car has swung around, so that the side of it – not the front – is against the dyke. Steam or smoke is rising. I try to open my door before realising that of course I can't open it because it's pressed against the fucking dyke, isn't it? The fucking stupid stupid fucking dyke. Fucking hell. I blink the blood out of my eyes. Wait.

I touch my forehead. I've been bleeding. Have I hit my head? I look around.

It's dark outside.

How long have I been here? I must have been sitting here for *hours*. There's blood on the steering wheel. I wasn't even going that fast, I *wasn't—*

I throw myself into the passenger seat and open the passenger door. After a moment's wriggling I forget trying to get out in any kind of conventional way and just crawl, walking along the ground with my hands and flopping once I've freed my legs. My left leg feels hot and swollen.

I lie on my back for a moment. The sky above and to the east is clear and purple and full of stars. To the west – my left – the stars are diminished by the orange light of Sellafield.

The grass is frosty underfoot. I'm moving very slowly. Every step with my left foot is agony. I can smell smoke from open fires roaring in the hearths of people's homes. Threads of the scent are winding their way through the cold night air, presumably from the various farms scattered around. Autumn has always been my favourite season. It has the best smells. I associate autumn with Granddad; I think it was his favourite season, too. I remember going out looking for conkers with him, and the bonfires, of course. And he used to help me make a Guy every year, and take me out to the fireworks. He knew all the neighbours and it was a social thing for him as much as anything. Cinder toffee. Early frosts. Raking up dead leaves and jumping in the piles. That smell of woodsmoke and coal. Walking the dog across misty morning fields. That was before the dog got old and died. That was before Granddad and Grandma got too old to walk far. When I was little, when they still looked after me, and not the other way around.

I am presumably not being chased or they would have had me by now. The tooth man must just have been prepared to defend the Candle. The Candle is true to its word after all, it appears.

PART FIVE

. . . one of my favourite writers, Hugh Walpole. He set most of his *Herries Chronicles* in Cumbria, and there was one line in the first book which always struck me as truth, and which I have never forgotten:

'The mountains close us in. You will find every-thing here, sir. God and the Devil both walk on these fields.'

You really can find everything there, and there is indeed a darkness that I have not really addressed. But there is a darkness everywhere, is there not? The darkness we both currently face is certainly located far away from those mountain-fast fields. Now I know that neither you nor I are as religious as our parents, and I dont mean to suggest that I really do believe in God or the Devil walking around like ordinary men — I dont, not at all. But there is darkness and light, and there is great power amidst those mountains and lakes and rivers and trees. I cannot explain it very well. I think it is something you have to experience. Maybe, one day, I will take you there, and you shall. I would very much like to start a family with you, my love, somewhere far away from the cities and the smoke and the remnants of this war — somewhere safe.

Please, please, please write to me as soon as you are able. You are all that keeps me going.

Your ever-loving Herb.

CHAPTER TWENTY-FOUR

The road, when I reach it, is quiet, but I know traffic normally drives here all night long: taxis from Gosforth running to Whitehaven and back; boy-racers from the villages and valleys making the most of the nocturnal hours. Right now, though, I can't hear any cars. I cross over and then set off walking down the side of the road, heading south. I say walking, but it's too slow to be walking, and too unbalanced; it's more a kind of hopping.

I can still hear the sounds from Newton Manor. Amidst the agonised howling there is something else bubbling away – laughter, I am pretty sure. Though it is not as loud as the screams. I might be imagining the sound of somebody laughing – maybe I'm laughing to myself. I'm so tired, and my brain isn't working properly, I know that much. It has done something to enable me to endure this pain, and maybe in doing so it has lost something. I could very well be laughing myself . . . but the laughter is male; it's faint, and male.

I turn around, suddenly wondering if Phillip or Gabe or one of the Johns is walking behind me, but they're not, there's nobody there, just the grey road disappearing beneath dark hedgerows. I watch for a moment in case somebody – some giggling man – is about to emerge from the darkness.

I can still hear it, beneath the screaming.

The first car I see is heading north and is no use to me. I need to go south. I need to go back to Ravenglass.

There is another car, this one coming from behind me, from the north, moving fast. The road ahead is bathed in light. I stick my arm out and turn around, only to be near-blinded by the full-beam headlamps, and near deafened by the car horn as the driver holds it down and swerves around me. The driver releases the horn only to hit it again once more, twice more, three times more as the red glow of the taillights recedes.

It's to be expected, I suppose. I don't know what I look like: a risen corpse, probably, somebody who died in a car accident, back from the dead. I'm covered in mud and blood and leaves, and I can barely walk. My dreads must look like entrails, or a broken brain hanging out. And anybody who's seen the local news – or is it national news yet? – will probably know that tonight is not a good night to go picking up hitchhikers. Will they? What will people know or understand or believe?

I keep on going. I suppose I'm hoping for somebody irresponsible, somebody who doesn't give a fuck about anything going on in the world. There are usually plenty of such people around.

Another car heading south ignores me completely, as does the next.

I'm just past the Gosforth-Seascale crossroads when somebody finally screeches to a stop. The car is a long, low red thing – it looks expensive. Sellafield workers, probably. When I approach, I see that the passenger seat is occupied, so I open the rear door and get in the back. The car smells of weed.

'Thank you,' I say. 'Thank you so much. I'm a bit muddy, I'm sorry.'

The driver – a handsome boy in his late teens or early twenties, with dark, styled hair and an angular, clean-shaven face – twists in his seat and appraises me conspicuously. He is wearing a heavy-looking black coat, buttoned up to the neck. The passenger looks at me too. She is beautiful, with long blonde hair and huge pale-blue eyes. She has her bare feet up on the dashboard and her white dress has ridden up her thighs. She is wearing a thick, soft leather jacket that looks too big for her. It's not enough to keep her warm.

Something tells me that the boy has just removed his hand from between her legs.

Although surely they wouldn't have picked me up in that case? Both of them wear small, slightly bemused smiles.

'No worries,' the boy says. His voice is slow, deep, slightly slurred.

'What happened to you?' the girl asks.

'I was out walking,' I say, 'and I got lost in the fields. I fell over climbing a wall.'

My own voice sounds strange to me, defeated. I have rehearsed the line again and again in my head, but hadn't thought to say it out loud. The boy and the girl just stare at me. 'I got lost in the fields,' I say, again. I thought it a pretty foolproof story as I dragged myself along the road, but now I'm not so sure it holds up.

The girl's smile widens. 'Well, there are a lot of them about.'

'Yeah,' I say, and laugh.

'Where do you want to go?' the boy asks.

'Ravenglass.'

'That's no problem.'

'Where are you going?' I ask.

'Swimming,' responds the girl.

'Oh, right,' I say. 'Where?'

'Some lake,' says the boy, 'or river.'

'Won't the water be too cold? It's winter.'

They both look at me for a moment longer and then turn back to face forwards.

'It will be very cold, yes,' the boy says.

'Do you want to come with us?' asks the girl.

The black water, the clear sky, the mountains still and

implacable and a fire on the shore and this beautiful strange boy and beautiful strange girl laughing, splashing, swimming, diving down into unknowable depths, their naked skin gleaming whitely through the liquid beneath me, and nothing else in the world, no other people or places, nothing – apart from graceful, otherworldly animals that might join us to drink at the water's edge; gentle creatures who know that we don't mean them any harm. There would be a small waterfall we could sit or stand beneath. We could close our eyes and let the waterfall run over our heads. The water would be icy and would eventually numb us through.

'No thanks,' I say, looking away. My eyes drift downwards and I see for the first time that my leg is so swollen that my jeans are bulging outwards.

Then we are away, and the car zips down the road at a speed beyond any I've ever travelled at, and the boy and the girl are laughing at something, I don't know what, but I know it's not me. The laughter is not malicious; it's warm and cold at the same time. It's inviting, it's delirious. The girl's window is open and her hair is streaming outwards in the wind.

We burn past Harecroft, tear through Hallsenna, Holmrook and Saltcoats. They ignore the obvious turn-offs for Wasdale and Eskdale, which is where I presume they were going, but I let them take me to my destination. They're going so fast that it won't take them any time at all to retrace their steps and disappear amongst the tiny roads and crystal waterways of the quieter valleys.

When we get to Ravenglass, the boy slows down.

'Here,' I say, as we pass The Tup, 'just here is fine, thank you. Thank you so much.'

'Not at all,' says the boy. 'Ravenglass is a strange place to come at this time of night.'

'A strange place to come any time,' I say.

He nods at that, and the girl laughs again.

I get out of the car and brush away some of the mud I've left on the seat.

'Enjoy your swimming,' I say.

They both look at me and smile broadly.

'We will,' says the girl. 'Goodnight.'

'Goodnight,' I say, and I close the car door. I watch as they turn around and race off back to the A595.

After the relative warmth of the car, I am shivering.

Ravenglass feels even more like a village at the end of the world now. The stillness is absolute; apart from one small metal gate creaking forlornly, nothing is moving. I watch the gate as it moves slowly on its hinges. I hobble over to it. It's about waist-high, two feet across. When closed, it would bar the entrance to the front yard of one of the road-side houses. It's painted white, though the paint has bubbled and flaked off, and the metal beneath is rusting in the salt air, so it's more orange than white. It's a sad little thing.

I push it closed and fasten the latch, so it can't move or creak any more.

CHAPTER TWENTY-FIVE

I'm in the caravan packing a bag, a backpack, just with basic things – purse, underwear, toothbrush – when somebody knocks at the door. It's Gabe, probably, wondering where his mum is. And I want to get Gabe, I want him to come with me, anyway. And John Senior too, for that matter.

I put the bag on my back and open the door and in front of me is a man holding a great big sharp metal object. He looks familiar, but he's lifting the metal thing up and bringing it down and I fall backwards to get out of the way, and it's an anchor, one of those little razor-sharp anchors, and he's coming up the steps with it and in the light of the caravan I see his face and it's a big mess, all scabs and grit. Overall it looks the same colour as that awful green coat. It's Phillip.

He's unable to lift the anchor quickly, but it's heavy and

sharp and still lethal. He swings it around himself and I feel it skim the top of my head, snagging a dread and yanking me to the side.

He grunts. He stinks.

I crawl past him as he gathers the anchor to himself again and slip out of the door. I'm on my feet, but I still can't move very fast; every time I put weight on my left foot the pain rises up my leg and darkens my vision, threatening to knock me out. If a doctor saw me he would tell me that I need a cast. He would say that trying to use my leg would make it worse; that I shouldn't even be trying to move it; that if I keep on putting weight on it, even only briefly, I would most likely be damaging it long-term.

But Phillip must be in more pain than me. I look over my shoulder briefly and he is only shambling along. If I could move properly, he would be laughable; as it is, the whole situation is pathetic. His camera is hanging from his neck and it bounces against his belly as he lurches after me. I'm gaining though; putting distance between us.

I limp on down the road towards the beach. I don't know where I'm going. The houses have broken windows now and there are shapes moving in the shadows. My plan was to get Gabe, get to the Platts', ask John to drive, but now . . .

When I look back again, Phillip is holding the anchor like an axe. It's basically a razored claw on the end of a long metal handle.

I pass the chandlery on my left. The door is hanging open. No doubt that's where Phillip found his weapon.

I don't look ahead as I walk, or behind me; I just look down. It's a long way to the water's edge – a long way for me in this condition, I mean – and the tide still has a long way to go out. I match my breathing to the shushing sound of the small breakers. Phillip's panting and grunting and the dragging of his feet fall into place too; they fall into the rhythm.

The sea is dark blue and glittering beneath the clear sky. I pass between upturned boats, barnacles clinging to their hulls. I imagine I can hear the creatures clicking and squirming beneath their shells. I am so cold – so, so cold. I am leaving strange tracks in the sand: footprints with my right foot and sweeping arcs with my left. It is easier if I don't try to lift it and put it back down; instead I just shift it and then let it take my weight for the shortest, sharpest of moments. The sand looks blue in the starlight: blue sand and a blue sea and a starry sky. This can be a beautiful place.

I can feel and hear him getting closer.

I am heading south, and also outwards, towards the water. A plan is slowly forming; I know what I want to find now, but I don't know exactly where it is.

An almost sub-audible thump hits me, and I feel a vibration through my feet as the ground shakes. The anchor landing in the sand, next to me? I turn around on my good

leg, expecting to see him standing there, his split face drib-
bling blood, having reached me before I wanted him to.

But the space around me is deserted. Phillip is still
coming, but the anchor is in his hands, not the ground.

I turn back around, and there's another thump, another
vibration.

It's Eskmeals – the weapons-testing station. They do some
of their work through the night.

I keep on trudging. I keep on watching the sand.

With the next vibration there's an explosion out at sea:
a bright white light that flares briefly and then fades away.
For a moment the stars disappear and the sea is lit up. I'm
closer to it than I realised. And I haven't yet found what
I'm looking for.

I change direction so that I'm parallel to the shore, and
continue heading south. I know I'll find it eventually, but
it needs to be soon, before it's too late.

I'm pretty sure that I'm into the prohibited area now.
I'm past the red dotted line on the map, the weapons-testing
zone. That's incidental, though; that's not really why I'm
here. I could maybe have found what I'm looking for nearer
the village, or even in the estuary. But I didn't.

One foot in front of the other, and repeat, again and
again and again. Life is just moving around in different
ways, that's all it is. You just have to keep moving in this
way or that way, one foot up and then down and then the
next. Move your tongue and your teeth and lips to say the

right words. Enter the right rooms at the right times. Move your eyes over the right documents. All the time, just move.

That feeling, my grandmother used to say it was somebody walking over your grave. A shudder and tingle that ripples across your whole body, apropos of nothing. I stop moving. It happens again.

For a brief moment I am standing back at the end of the road by the chandlery, looking out over the beach. And in the distance, just visible, is a figure – two figures, both small and black against the shimmering sea. It's a vision of Phillip, and I happen to be in the background. Phillip is laughing quietly to himself.

My stomach clenches, hard, and I'm seeing back out of my own eyes again. I start to shake. I know what he's capable of. I knew it would come to this, but I didn't want it to. I didn't. What will he do to me?

I press on. I want to go faster. I look back over my shoulder – I know I shouldn't, I should just carry on, but I can't help it.

To the east, over the bulk of the rising land, dawn is breaking.

I keep going. How many times have I said those words to myself: *just keep going*? Ignore the demon at your back; keep going. Just keep going. He will catch you, yes, but not here. Just. Keep. Going.

And maybe he is a demon of some sort, one of the creatures, because he *was* dead, I'm sure of it. Maybe the Candle resurrected him, since it knew it would get no more blood from me. Maybe the Candle decided to break its promise after all.

I can hear him – although I don't know what the sound is. A keening, maybe: it is a mocking sound, but not a sound a human would ever make any more. It is a battle-cry, an animal noise, a ululation, a taunt: *I am going to make you hurt.* It goes on and on. *I am going to eat you from the inside out.* The sound drifts across the blue sand like an alien wind. *I am going to do things to you that you cannot even imagine. I am going to keep you alive.* There is laughter in it. *What I did to the Geordie will be nothing next to what I will do to you, Edie Grace.*

I try to run, and my breath comes in sobs. The sand here is shining like metal. There is nothing ahead of me now but the sand and the sea and the sky, and behind me, there is nothing but him.

I look back again. I can't help it.

He is a tall, black figure against the pink-tinged sand. His shoulders are hunched slightly. He is unbalanced and ungainly. He moves erratically, as if he is not just stumbling but sometimes jumping too. He zigzags, falls to all fours and uses his hands to lever himself upright again. It's as if his pain is diminishing. He's getting faster. This has to be the Candle's work. *You wanted Phillip Banks.* Phillip is reflected in the metallic sand and so there are two of him leaping and lurching. He shimmers in the bending light.

The sky above him to the east is lighter now – an extraordinary colour – though the sun has not yet risen.

He is barrelling, albeit in an erratic trajectory, and I am—I am not even walking. I am hobbling, limping, trudging, hopping. I am a pitiful human tangle of flesh and bone and hair. I am a disgrace, a failure. I have failed. He will catch me and have me here on this sand and I will die and he will live. For ever. He will live for ever.

Keep going, Edie. *Keep going.*

I keep going.

His voice is all around me now.

I keep going.

The tide is still going out. The sea is retreating from him.

There is another thump, another flash: another weapon has been tested. I imagine a group of men in white coats and thick spectacles standing around the window in some safe bunker, applauding.

I keep going, but now I change direction so that I'm heading diagonally to the south, towards the sea.

I can hear him shouting and laughing and keening. And there are animal sounds, grunts and roars and howls. He sounds close.

The sand ahead of me is now turning pink, and the sea beyond that. Pink fingers are reaching through the sky above me towards the maritime horizon, where the stars still gleam in a deep purple darkness.

Keep going.

The sand here is wet. Have I found it?

I keep going. My feet are not leaving tracks any more; instead, the sand reshapes itself as I pass, filling my prints.

I think I've found it.

I keep going.

I'm sobbing now. Tears are spilling down my cheeks to land on the shining surface through which I'm sinking. I think about the Elsewhere, and permeable boundaries. I would like to travel infinitely.

I keep going.

I have not taken the necessary steps, though. I have discovered I am not willing to do whatever it takes.

The sand is like a desperate, clingy lover, pawing at me, unhappy to let me go. It's creeping beneath my jeans, pressing against the skin of my ankles. It's bitterly cold, but I have to keep going. The more you struggle the more it pulls you in, but if it's there to pull me in then it's there to pull him in too.

I don't dare look back now. I will have to at some point, but first I need to get further out, further in. Moving is getting harder and harder as the sand gets softer and softer.

Keep going.

Behind me he laughs and laughs. The wet splash of his footsteps is louder. 'Edie!' he shouts, elongating my name with a shriek. His voice is all bubbly. 'Look what you did, Edie!'

I pretend to trip and throw myself forwards. I don't want

him to know what I know. The fall happens slowly. I see my body from outside of myself, my hands in front of my face, my body completely straight, even my legs unbent. I describe an arc. I am as rigid as a piece of wood.

I won't ever hit the ground. Time will stop like this.

Or time won't stop, and I will sink right through the ground and just keep on sinking, and everything around me will be cold and wet and pink and granular.

My arms splash into the sand and it spatters against my closed eyelids, my cheeks, my lips: *so cold*. More laughter erupts from behind me, pealing against the sky.

Words flit through my brain: morning is breaking.

I start to crawl. Weight distribution is the thing, in theory. It's like crawling over something submerged just beneath the surface of a pool. Something gradually getting lower and lower. It laps against my face. I pull myself along with my bruised knees, with my bruised elbows.

I'm shaking. My right arm gives way and my face splashes into the sandy water and it floods my mouth. It's grainy, foul, coating my tongue, and I can't spit. My stomach heaves, a rolling wave of revulsion originating in my gut and gathering speed as it approaches my mouth. I vomit up acid.

I'm sinking.

The sand is relentless, unthinking, tireless. It won't ever give up. It's not a living thing; it's not something you can beat. This was a bad idea. I'll drown in the land and he will skate across the top, grab my legs . . . any moment now those rotten fingers will fasten around my flesh.

No.

Keep going.

I raise my head up and blink. There is no beach any more, no sky, just a vibrant pink expanse stretching out beyond me, shot through with liquid ripples of light and shade. The sand goes on and on and eventually curves up to become the sky. There is no visible distinction between the ground and the air; it's a uterine continuum in which I'm suspended, floundering, looking down and seeing only the same colour, the same texture as that of the sky. Pale rose clouds float beneath me, between my disappearing hands. I must be heading towards the sea, but I don't know. I have never seen the beach like this before – if this *is* even the beach.

The whole strange world is suddenly shaking with a howl, a victorious howl, joyful and inhuman at the same time. It's not a distant sound; it is coming from right behind me.

I start to drag myself forwards again and the howling ends abruptly.

'You can't crawl fast enough or far enough, Edie Grace,' he says. He is not shouting now; he is talking. He is close enough to just talk. But the shouting and wailing has cost him, tired him out, and he has to pause between every couple of words to draw breath.

I shut my eyes and keep crawling.

'Give up,' he says, 'I've caught you.'

I keep my eyes shut and I keep going, but my legs are shaking violently, waiting for his hand, or the anchor, or his mouth, even.

There is a sudden flurry of movement at my back, the sound of splashing and sucking, and a roar. Something has closed on my left foot like a bear trap and my whole body spasms. The pain isn't just a sensation; it's something alive inside of me burrowing everywhere at once, as if looking for a way out.

I roll to my left so that I'm on my back and there is another burst of pain from my foot, which stays where it is, with my toes pointing into the sand. Pointing the *wrong way*, gripped by his hand – his *right* hand. His stained, long-nailed fingers have my ankle trapped. I look at him. The anchor is resting over his left shoulder.

He is submerged up past his waist. He is a dark green and red torso, rising from the coral land, and his blood is still fresh on his chest, still wet. It flows out into the liquid around us; it must be new blood; he must still be bleeding. His face is twisted into a misshapen mask. He is not struggling against the sand now. He knows what it is.

I look at his fingers clasped around my swollen ankle. I've only got one chance. It's the thumb I need to go for.

I lean forwards, and dig my nails into his thumb, hard and deep, and rake them backwards, and he lets out a yelp and involuntarily lets go, and I jerk my legs back towards me, away from his grasping hands. I shuffle further back, away from him. I'm aflame with burning white pain from my broken ankle, but I'm compartmentalising it, closing my eyes to it, burying it deeply.

He leans forwards to grab me, but he cannot reach. Instinctively he tries to move, but then he stops himself.

'Quicksand,' I say. I roll back onto my front and crawl further away, then I turn over again and sit up.

He stares at me, his frown deepening. He is the only solid thing around; everything else is running together. His eyes are burning deep inside that foul face. He says something unintelligible, something garbled; I don't know what, but it sounds guttural and vile.

Then he throws his head back and roars, opening his mouth wide, casting his arms up above his head. He looks like he is being born from the ground, slathered in viscera and screaming.

I start crawling again, this time around him, being sure to keep my distance.

'Bitch,' he spits. 'Fool. Cow. Mare. Cunt. This is *my* land, Edie Grace. *My home.*'

My body is ruined. It is an accident of broken bones and frayed muscle. My clothes and skin are invisible beneath a layer of sand. I'm a mudhopper, a lugworm, an alien invertebrate on some other world. I am going to die. But first . . .

I'm moving behind him and he is trying to turn around to face me, twisting in the slop. He can't bring the anchor down behind himself, but he tries anyway and it splashes into the quicksand.

I grab it and pull it away.

He screams and writhes and thrashes around, which makes him sink further. I'm directly behind him now and he can't see me without turning his head to the side. I crawl towards him, still trying to keep my weight even, keeping the anchor low. I get closer and closer and he is reaching backwards, but in trying to do both that and keep his hands above the sand his reach is diminished, and his control, and his strength.

I kneel and grab the anchor in both hands. I hold it firm and breathe in deeply. He's moving around too much, and in a horrible way, an insect-like way. I found a kitten once that had been run over on the road, outside my grandparents' house. The car had just squashed the top of its head and its body was twitching, trapped in the same repetitive movement, like a stuck DVD. That's what Phillip is like: animalistic, insectile . . . I don't know, he's somehow base and desperate. He knows what's coming, that's what it is.

I exhale and inhale again, and then I slam the anchor down onto the back of his head and the claw of it sticks right in. That will have to do – I can't do it again. He screams and wriggles and I blink and fall backwards. I keep shuffling away. He moves what is left of his head, ever so slightly, and I lose control of my bladder and scream. I scream and . . .

I am out of the quicksand. I am lying on the firm beach, on my front, facing inland. The sun is higher in the sky. Unconsciousness is receding like mist or sleep. I must have lost it.

When I look he's still out there. His blood-red remains rise from the sand like a statue, a remnant from some long-gone civilisation, something uncovered by time. My vision is blurry and he is indistinct against the shining sea, and getting increasingly so as my eyes fill up, and he seems to disappear and then come back, disappear and then come back, as my sight wavers and returns.

As I watch, there's a soft thump from the south and then a low whistle and then the faint vibration of a distant explosion, a bomb or another weapon, something violent disturbing the shallow estuary waters, the wet sand, the surface of the land itself.

Chapter Twenty-Six

'I had this feeling, once,' I say, 'actually, I can pinpoint it: it was when I was coming up here. I came up here when my grandparents died, after finding these letters Granddad wrote to Grandma. He grew up here, but he met Grandma in London and then he went to war, and a year or two after he got back Mum was born. And they ended up staying there. I can't work out why, not after reading the letters. But I suppose people change. Priorities change. Anyway.'

Gabe doesn't say anything. He keeps his eyes on the road. It's a clear bright morning and we're heading south over the white-frosted fells towards the M6 – in a stolen car and everything, like we're in an action film. But neither of us feels excited. Above everything, we feel tired. After the M6 I don't know where we're going. I'm smoking, though I don't remember lighting the cigarette.

'After Grandma died, I resolved I would never settle down

with anyone,' I say. 'People find that hard to understand, but I think it's to do with my mum as well: I don't want to end up like her, so sad it ruins you. I'm happy on my own. At least, I was, before all this.' I gesture down at my leg, though that's not quite what I'm referring to.

'We should go to a hospital,' Gabe says. He is struggling to hold it together, now he knows about Maria, but he is strong. He is crying, but it's a strange, repressed kind of crying, like the tears are forcing their way out, like they're leaking through pinprick holes in a dam.

He's probably right about the hospital.

'Every time you looked at your love, you'd imagine them old, senile, dying,' I say. 'That's how it would be for me, anyway. I would look at him and imagine one of us dying, and then the other. When I was little, I used to pray before bed every night: I'd pray for God to make everybody in the world die at exactly the same time. I started off just praying that me and my grandparents would all die at the same time, but then I realised that there would be people who would miss us, so I widened it out, listing all the people I could think of, until finally I just settled on everybody.'

Gabe doesn't reply. He wipes his eyes, and every time he takes his hand off the wheel the car swerves a little bit. I don't think he's been sleeping much since he glassed Phillip. He is probably too tired to drive.

I felt the moment that we escaped the Candle's dominion. As we passed Waberthwaite, an unpleasant pressure started to build across my mind, and then after a moment it snapped, and it was gone. As if I'd broken an elastic band.

I worked out then that if the centre of the Candle's realm was Greycroft, and the edge of it was now at Waberthwaite, it would encompass Sellafield, Seascale, Gosforth and the beginning of Wasdale as well as Ravenglass. And that's only half of it – the other half would be exercising its influence out over the sea. That's assuming the Candle's domain is circular; an expansion of the stone circle it started with. Circles within circles, like the tattoos on the back of the Candle's hands. Like a great eye looking up from the land itself.

The wider world will start to notice that something is wrong very soon. What they'll find back there, I don't want to know.

The sky is grey today, a very pale grey. I look in the rear-view mirror and see the Johns are both looking out of their side windows. John Senior is the same colour as the sky and trembling slightly and he keeps turning and looking out of the back windscreen. He's muttering about the fey. John Junior is just sitting there with his hands over his face. I didn't really want to pick him up but John Senior wouldn't leave without him. I don't know if they're okay; I mean, there's a chance that they've been affected like Pitbull was, like others were, and they might yet start showing signs. But I only saw that happen to the contractors; people new to the area. Maybe the stones granted some protection to those of us who've lived near them for a period of time. Maybe the Candle's powers affected visitors first – its rabid desire for its own old land manifesting itself as some kind of bigotry.

'What was it?' Gabe asks.

'What?'

'What was the feeling? You started talking about a feeling?'

'Oh.' I think back. 'Oh yes, on my way up to Cumbria, driving north up the M6. I don't remember there being any sound and the motorway stretched out straight ahead of me. It rose gradually and I could see a long way along it. Everything around was flat and the sky was blue, but it was like a fake blue, like an IKEA blue. There were no other cars heading the same way as me; just big high-sided lorries, generic ones with no logos, all white or blue, with straps flapping. They were probably travelling fast, but they must have all been travelling at the same speed because they looked stationary, relative to each other. There they were, one after the other, filling the left-hand lane and the two middle lanes. I felt as if I was part of a tribe, as if we were nomads, a caravan, traversing some great desert. We were all going to the same place and we would all turn off our engines together in a new future world. All humans would migrate to this place, to this same future. I was excited: the lorries were all full of building materials and we were going to build something magnificent once we reached our destination: something permanent, for all humankind that came afterwards. The sun gleamed off the metal bits of the lorries and off the road too, as if that were also metal, and we drove on through the silence and the heat, looking for just the right place and time in which to build our monument.

'That was the feeling – a kind of positivity about the future – but I can only think we never found it – the right place to build, I mean. And I don't know what we'd build, anyway, even if we did find the right place. If we ever did.'

While I'm speaking, an image forms in my mind: a black stone, and then, further away, another, and another, and another, and more, arranged in a circle, and they're weathered and ancient – older than any of us will ever be.

Acknowledgements

Firstly, infinite thanks to Beth for being so patient, supportive, and understanding, and for giving me the time and space to write. I can't thank you enough. Thank you to Jake, our son, for being such a delightful baby. Thank you to our families, for helping out in countless ways since Jake's birth (and before, for that matter). Thank you also to Nick Royle, friend and agent, for honest feedback and good advice at every juncture. Thank you to Jo Fletcher and Nicola Budd at Jo Fletcher Books for everything you've done to guide this book through to publication, for your experience and your professionalism, and for being such good company. Enormous thanks also to the members – past and present – of Northern Lines; Jenn Ashworth, Zoe Lambert, Emma Unsworth, Claire Massey, Sally Cook, Andrew Hurley, Maria Roberts, Russ Litten, and Socrates Adams. The workshops and discussions have been invaluable, as have all the Sunday afternoon pints. It's an honour to be part of such a formidably talented writing group, and a pleasure too. And finally, thank you – of course – to the readers.